"We need to talk, Officer Roberts."

"I have to go. It's a family matter. It has nothing to do with this case, Sergeant."

Nick wanted to believe her. The problem was the fear he saw in her dark brown eyes. "What *does* it have to do with, then?"

Sarah looked around uncomfortably. "My sister's... safety. I can't talk about it."

"Not here, you mean? Not to me?"

She looked him in the eye and he knew something was wrong. "Just trust me—you don't need to know."

Nick felt the knife in his back again. Except this petite woman was standing right in front of him. "You're leaving before finishing reports. I'd say I need to know. You may have FBI credentials, but it's my duty to make sure you know how to survive on the streets. And I can assure you a distracted police officer may be a danger to herself and her partner."

The silence between them lengthened. Her voice softened. "I wouldn't do that to you." She glanced up at him. "Never."

Books by Carol Steward

Love Inspired Suspense

*Guardian of Justice
In His Sights
*Badge of Honor

*In the Line of Fire

Love Inspired

There Comes a Season
Her Kind of Hero
Second Time Around
Courting Katarina
This Time Forever
Finding Amy
Finding Her Home
Journey to Forever

CAROL STEWARD

To Carol Steward, selling a book is much like riding a roller coaster—every step of the process, every sale brings that exhilarating high. During the less exciting times, she's busy gathering ideas and refilling her cup. Writing brings a much-needed balance to her life, since she has her characters share lessons she has learned, as well.

When she's not working at the University of Northern Colorado, you can usually find her spending time with her husband of over thirty years, writing and thanking God she survived raising her own three children, to reap His rewards of playing with her adorable grandchildren.

Throughout all the different seasons of life, God has continued to teach Carol to turn to Him. She has also learned to simplify her life and appreciate her many blessings—His gift of creativity, sharing her love for God with readers and setting an example of what God can do when we say, "Yes, God, take me, shape me, use me." To find out more about Carol's slightly crazy life and her books, visit her Web site at www.carolsteward.com.

BADGE
of HONOR

Carol Steward

Steeple
Hill®

Published by Steeple Hill Books™

STEEPLE HILL BOOKS

Steeple
Hill®

ISBN-13: 978-0-373-44306-2
ISBN-10:   0-373-44306-4

BADGE OF HONOR

www.SteepleHill.com

Printed in U.S.A.

For to this you have been called,
because Christ also suffered for you, leaving you
an example, that you should follow in His steps.
He committed no sin; no guile was found on his
lips. When he was reviled, he did not revile in
return; when he suffered, he did not threaten;
but he trusted to him who judged justly.
—*I Peter* 2:21–23

This book could not have come together without the support of many dear friends and loved ones. First, for understanding that it kills me to miss the chance to spend time with all of you. Know that you're always near my thoughts, even when I'm writing. You'll see what I mean. Second, for not only understanding, but helping me through the rough spots, whether it's cooking dinner—again— or a massage, or helping me throw out a scene and make it better. You're all the greatest inspiration I could ever ask for.

Again, to my editor, Melissa—
I can't thank you enough.

To my wonderful husband, Dave. Thanks for taking a chance on me and never letting me give up on my dreams. Thirty years and counting!

To my daughter, Sarah, and her husband, who are both a true blessing to me, and whose real-life determination to forever live up to being the oldest breathed life into a cookie-cutter character.
God bless you both.

ONE

Nick Matthews marched into the precinct, a wave of silence rippling in his wake. His life had changed forever. Even here, with the men and women who had been his friends and defended his life, the shadow of doubt tainted his return. He wouldn't be able to repair the damage to his honor overnight, but he wasn't about to walk away.

Fighting crime was his life.

Nick noticed a petite woman walk into the building next to him and turned to investigate. Opening the door to the administrative wing of the police station, he held it as she hurried through.

"Thank you," she said, tossing her full hair over her shoulder.

He nodded, trying to turn off the guilt of admiring a pretty woman. He wasn't committed to anyone anymore. Ronda had taken care of that with one swift judgment.

With his conscience cleared, Nick turned to introduce himself, stopped when the FBI seal on her navy polo shirt stole his interest.

His adrenaline kicked into high gear, like it did when he was working a case. Why was the FBI here? What was she investigating? Or should he ask *who?*

Before he could say anything, she turned down the hall toward the shift commander's office and disappeared without another word.

Nick entered the men's locker room preoccupied with thoughts of the woman in the FBI shirt. As he made his way through, he heard someone say, "There was another assault last night."

Nick listened, wondering if they had a serial criminal on their streets. Maybe that was why "Miss FBI" was here.

"Was it the same M.O. as the rape last spring…?" The officer's voice faded the minute he saw Nick.

"No, didn't get that far. Three students walked by and scared him off." The lower voice was easy to identify. Jared Daniels.

Steeling himself against the dreaded silence, Nick wondered how the chief thought returning to patrol duty rather than to his position as detective would build trust again. But Nick didn't voice his questions. Those were his orders.

"Hey there, Matthews, welcome back," Officer Jeremy Logan said as he walked past.

Nick nodded. "Thanks, Jeremy. It's good to be here." He fielded a greeting or two, and more than a few skeptical glares from other officers. No one wanted to be associated with a troublemaker, let alone a cop suspected of being on the take. Lockers clanged shut as the whispers turned to silence. One by one, a half-dozen men slipped out of the room in quick succession.

He silently repeated Isaiah 43:2, the verse that had gotten him through this ordeal. "When you pass through deep waters, I will be with you: your troubles will not overwhelm you." Some days, like today, Nick questioned how much tribulation God thought he could handle. His own opinion was obviously very different from God's.

Opening his locker, Nick took a quick inventory. He hadn't been in here for weeks, and hadn't worn his uniform since he'd moved to the investigative unit three years ago.

Ignoring the silence was impossible.

These officers had been like family. He couldn't believe any one of them would think he'd have gone along with anyone on the force selling confiscated drugs. Worse yet was the implication that three officers had been involved in the underground drug ring. So if it wasn't Nick, they were still looking for one more culprit.

Nick noticed Sean Randall hurry in, stopping to open a locker nearby.

"Hey, Matthews, how're you doing?" he asked, as if he'd forgotten Nick wore a scarlet letter on his badge.

"Doing okay," he said simply. He wasn't about to jump in and make the same mistakes again. Figuring out who he could trust was going to take time, no matter how good a detective he'd been. He couldn't interrogate each of his colleagues.

Time.

Patience.

Prayers.

Vic Taylor and Jed Tate had been convicted and were awaiting sentencing. Even with the promise of a lighter sentence, they wouldn't give up any other names, which left a whole lot of suspicion running rampant.

Nick didn't want to believe another officer on the force was involved. That those two had been working drug cases, forming a drug ring, was unbelievable.

He had to get to the bottom of this.

This is not a demotion. It's not even discipline. Much as he tried to convince himself of that, it wasn't working.

He pinned his badge and name tag to the shirt, then began putting on the required layers for traffic officers. The Kevlar vest and uniform shirt weren't nearly as comfortable as his plainclothes uniform, and he was pretty sure they hadn't been this snug last time he'd patrolled the streets, either.

Nick took the shirt off, checked for his name on the label ironed to the collar, to be sure someone hadn't switched them. When had he put on weight? He tugged the shirt across his chest to button it. He'd need to order the next size larger— soon. That, or buy a thinner vest. With the gang activity in the area on the rise, he wasn't about to take that chance. He sucked in and fastened the shirt, praying it held through the shift. *I look like a body builder trying to look buff,* he thought. *Just what I need tonight.*

"Put on a little weight since you left the streets, huh, Matthews?" Sean said with a laugh. "Welcome back."

"Thanks," he said gruffly. "It's all muscle. I've been working out in my time off."

"Yeah," Randall muttered, "Me, too. My wife says it's sympathy weight. She expects me to lose it as soon as the baby arrives."

"Your wife is pregnant?"

"That's right," Sean bragged. "Our first."

"Congratulations." Nick was stunned that Sean continued the conversation. He'd expected total silence. "When's the big day?"

"Doc says December 8. We'll see. Noelle's showing already." The officer practically blushed as Nick chuckled. Sean finished dressing and closed his locker. "We'll catch up later."

"Yeah, take it easy." Nick made the necessary adjustments to his duty belt, adding his handcuffs, baton and flashlight rings before making his way to the briefing room. He sat in the back row, trying to lie low. Hushed voices dropped to a deafening silence the minute he took his seat.

Nick knew what they were going through. He even knew what they were thinking. He'd never known what to say when an officer came back after being disciplined for breaking policy. Now he knew how it felt to be the one no one wanted to get too close to. He looked around, trying to place names with the new faces. He was pretty sure Captain Thomas had said his trainee was a female officer. There were two women here he didn't recognize. The FBI agent was nowhere in sight.

When the shift commander entered the room and stopped to say hello, Nick's hopes of staying invisible were blown to smithereens. He fought the urge not to slump in his chair, as he had in high school when a teacher embarrassed him by calling on him when he'd walked into class after the bell.

"Let's welcome Nick back to street patrol," the commander said, obviously trying to break the awkward tension in the room. "Congratulations on the outcome, Sergeant Matthews." That ominous cloud of silence broke when two officers joined the commander's clapping, and the rest reluctantly followed.

Once the murmur of voices returned to normal, the commander began the briefing. "We have changes to the Field Training Officer assignments. Sarah Roberts," he said as a deafening silence took over the room again. Thomas motioned toward the front row, where the petite woman who had walked in with Nick, stood, barely clearing the heads of the men sitting behind her. Her dark hair was neatly braided and she looked like a teenager waiting for a growth spurt to befall her. "Officer Roberts comes to Fossil Creek with ten years of FBI field experience. You'll spend the next four weeks training with your FTO Sergeant Matthews."

Nick figured every officer in the room was thinking the same thing he was—that Nick Matthews had a new watchdog.

Despite the annoyance, he nodded as Officer Roberts's glance met his. *It can't be the same Sarah Roberts who went to Fossil Creek High, could it?* As she took her seat, Nick struggled to focus on taking notes for the night's shift, BOLOs, outstanding warrants and cases to be mindful of—mainly the assault case from the night before. He struggled to keep his mind from drifting to the cute twin sister of his old basketball teammate.

He refused to look again. He forced himself to focus on the briefing as Captain Thomas went into detail on the BOLO.

"Be on the lookout for any suspicious activity near the campus," the captain explained as Nick struggled to link Sarah's assignment to the assault case.

"…second assault in the vicinity of the university last night. Suspect is described as five-ten, Caucasian, brown hair and medium build. It occurred between nine and ten last night near the fine arts building off Pine Street and Gateway Place. The university police have asked us to provide assistance with additional patrols of the area. This assault has several similarities to the rape that occurred last April. All units in that area double your patrols on the university perimeter until further notice."

Nick's mind wandered again, and he found himself wishing he was the detective on the case. Sitting on the fringes had never been his strength. But there was never a dull moment in a city of almost a hundred twenty thousand—thirty thousand more when the university was in session. Patrolling the streets had its perks, he realized—more action, fewer dead ends than in investigations. And it would be a lot more difficult to find out if someone still had it in for him.

After the briefing, he waited at the door to meet Officer Roberts. The majority of their colleagues used the opposite door, thus avoiding the need to address Nick.

"Nick Matthews," Sarah said confidently, as she stopped next to him and looked up. Her brown eyes, framed with long, dark lashes and high arched eyebrows, were filled with intrigue and intelligence, he noted as he offered his hand.

She was even shorter than she'd looked earlier and even prettier than she had been in high school. He'd guess she was just over five feet tall, the bulkiness of the Kevlar vest and boxy uniform slacks hiding any semblance of a womanly figure. Her face was a dead giveaway, however. Totally feminine. Her full lips would have been too much on most faces, but fit perfectly with her square jaw. He imagined she wore her hair in a thick braid because of the job. She probably didn't remember him—he'd been two years younger.

She looked him over once and nodded. "It's nice to finally meet you."

"You, too." He didn't want to think about what she meant by "finally."

How long were people going to question his word? His actions? His honor? And how was he supposed to erase that shadow of doubt two crooked officers had placed on his badge, when his superiors assigned a former FBI agent to be his new partner? *Heavenly Father, help me put the past behind me and move forward.*

TWO

Sarah saw the look of doubt in Nick's eyes. Whether it was skepticism that anyone so petite could be counted on as backup, or her experience with the FBI that he was upset about, she wasn't sure. She'd been in Fossil Creek for little over a month, and not one person yet seemed to believe she'd willingly left the Federal Bureau of Investigations to become a street officer. Sarah was growing tired of trying to prove herself.

"I'm sorry to ask to keep you waiting, but I really need to talk to the captain. I wasn't able to catch him earlier," she said, looking Nick in the eye. "It should only take a few minutes. Do you mind?"

He shrugged. "Be my guest."

She walked into their superior's office and closed the door. "Captain Thomas, do you have a minute?"

"Of course, my door's always open. I got your message on my way into the courtroom this morning. I can't tell you how sorry I am about your sister's attack last night. Is she okay?"

Sarah nodded. "She's pretty shaken up, but thankfully, the group of students came along and startled the suspect before he did anything more than scare her."

The captain frowned. "You don't have to stay and work tonight, if she wants you with her."

Sarah thanked him, but declined the offer. "She already had plans with a group of friends.... She thinks if she just goes on as usual, she'll be able to forget it happened. She doesn't want me hovering over her as a reminder."

"Well, if she does need you, call me personally. I'll make sure it's kept quiet," he stated.

"I wanted to thank you for not revealing that last night's victim was my sister."

"I wouldn't have, anyway," Thomas assured her. "But if at any point it becomes necessary to the investigation, you need to be prepared to talk to the detectives."

"Of course. I don't want anyone to think the case is getting preferential treatment because of me, but more than that, I want this guy caught and the charges to stick. If there's anything I can do to help the detectives catch him, just let me know." Sarah wasn't certain exactly how she was going to overcome the urge to take charge, but somehow she needed to stay out of it.

Captain Thomas nodded. "Right now, I think it's best to keep details as quiet as possible. The detectives are still trying to figure out if there is any connection between the rape last spring and your sister's attack. I'm curious about something, though. Didn't Detective Wang recognize you at the hospital?"

"He didn't seem to, sir."

Thomas looked at her, clearly puzzled. "Well, since he hasn't, we may as well let it play out naturally. I'm trusting you to stay out of the investigation, Roberts."

Sarah nodded. Somehow, she'd do it. "Definitely. In the investigator's defense, I'd like to say I make every effort to *not* look like a police officer when I'm off duty." She forced a smile that she didn't feel.

The captain laughed. "I'm going to have to push their observation skills a bit then. Maybe I could enlist your assistance, after the investigation is over."

Sarah studied her superior officer, not sure if he was serious or joking. "I have one more concern. It seems that my experience with the Bureau is a source of contention. It's not my imagination, is it?"

He shook his head. "Given time, the other officers will realize we're lucky to have you as one of us. I'm afraid the drug ring has set lots of imaginations running wild. No matter what we say, half the department is convinced we're still looking for another player in it."

"Time heals all wounds." She put her hand on the doorknob and paused. "Thank you for giving me a chance, Captain Thomas. Most places I applied threw out my application on the FBI merit alone. It's nice to be here in a smaller department."

"Their loss is Fossil Creek's gain. We need some new blood here. The drug ring made that very apparent. Now get out there and kick some life into Matthews, would you?"

Sarah found Nick Matthews leaning against the doorway to the officers lounge down the stairs, watching the latest news report of her sister's assault. "Have they mentioned the victim's name?" she asked him.

"Nah, they won't," he said, stepping forward. "Even the press has standards. Victim's rights are one of them. We ready to hit the streets?"

She nodded, noting he was taller than she remembered from high school. Ten years had changed both of them, she realized. His shirt looked two sizes too small, not that she minded. She just hoped it made it through the night without tearing.

Sarah went to get the police cruiser key from the board, and noticed it was gone. She turned to him. "You driving?"

"Nope, we'll see where Sergeant Donovan left off with your training." Matthews tossed the key to her, and she felt the butterflies in her stomach performing aerial stunts as he checked out an assault rifle from the gun vault. She followed, selecting her own.

"Great," she muttered as she inspected the car, securing their rifles and a ticket can in the trunk, while he scrutinized her every move. Her rotation with the first trainer had been a continuous reminder of the lesson she'd learned the hard way at the FBI—that men didn't like bossy women, whether it be at home or work. Nothing had been more difficult than discovering competency and self-reliance scared the marrying kind of man away, almost as fast as hearing she was a special agent for the FBI. "Suggestions?"

"Nope."

She got into the car and radioed dispatch that they were on duty and heading toward their assigned region of town. Thirty minutes later, Nick still hadn't said anything; he just silently scribbled on his notepad.

Sarah was getting desperate for some chatter, to the extent of being tempted to ask if he remembered her from high school. Anything to take her mind off Beth's attack and what he was writing down. Her sister refused to talk about it, and Nick didn't seem anxious to share, either. *Don't get pushy. Just do your job....*

Dispatch interrupted her thoughts. "Silent alarm

at Citizen's Bank on the corner of Birch and First Street."

"Three-eighteen copy," Sarah said, then put the mike back into the clip and turned toward the bank.

"It's not our area," Nick argued. "We serve as backup if needed."

Just as Nick predicted, the dispatcher sent another officer to respond, then added, "Three-eighteen stand by to back up if needed."

She could see the corner of Nick's mouth twitch. "It's only a block from our border," she said, trying to sound compliant. "I just thought we could help…."

"If it were a block farther east, we could respond. They'll call if they need backup, so stay in the area, in case. A little different from what you're used to, huh?"

She didn't need to get into an argument on her first night with a new training officer. She put the safety on her mouth before her attitude got her into trouble. "The FBI didn't serve as first responders on many calls, period."

"You miss it?"

"I was ready for a change. I always liked Fossil Creek, and with my sister in graduate school here, I decided it was a sign when I saw they were hiring."

"How long did your family live in Colorado?" he asked, sounding more like a detective than a partner. As if he couldn't be less interested if he tried.

"Ten years," she said, expecting him to ask the same question everyone else did—why had she left the FBI for a local police department? Nick didn't say anything, and the silence was deafening. She had to talk about something job related before she started worrying and talking about Beth. Experience and instinct told her she could trust Nick Matthews, but she wasn't sure she was ready to open up yet. She tried making conversation, to no avail. "I'm a little surprised to hear Fossil Creek is having such an explosion of gang and drug problems."

"Yeah, Greeley PD had to start a gang task force. They cracked down and pushed the gangs out. Now they're our problem. We need to give them a swift kick out of town, too, before they have a chance to get established here. Fortunately, they're not as organized as the West Coast gangs. Ours are mostly family and territory battles."

"What about the drugs?"

He didn't answer immediately, and Sarah realized she'd just put her foot in her mouth.

"Oh, I didn't mean… That came out wrong. Forget I said anything," she begged. "Nick, I'm sorry."

"Our drug task force does a great job. They work with the DEA and other Colorado agencies to get a leg up on the growing problems."

She felt blood rush to her face. "I didn't mean anything personal…."

Before she could continue, dispatch interrupted. "Three-eighteen, backup at Citizen's Bank. Suspect seen in back of the bank on foot, wearing a dark green shirt and baseball cap, Caucasian, dark hair, nylon stocking over his face. Headed toward University Drive."

"Three-eighteen copy," Sarah responded, happy to have something put a little distance between her and Nick. She turned on the flashing lights and siren and headed toward University Drive.

"Take the alley, just past the bus stop sign on the right," Nick instructed. "He's not going to stay on a main road if he's running."

"He could have a car or driver waiting."

"There's no parking on University. Take the alley," Nick ordered.

She made a last-minute turn into the laneway, annoyed to be given a command. Even more annoyed when he proved her wrong. She hurried toward the taillights of an orange car.

The suspect was stuffing a duffel bag into the passenger-side window and looked up, shocked to see them. He dived headfirst after the bag. The driver took off before his accomplice had pulled his legs inside.

Sarah called dispatch. "Suspect dived into a 1970 SS 454 Chevelle, Nebraska plates, William-Lincoln-Boy 783. That's WLB 783," she repeated. She followed with her lights flashing as the car sped away. If no one had been hurt at the bank, and no money taken, there was likely no need to risk the citizenry's safety with a high-speed pursuit. Sarah was hesitant to force a chase through rush hour traffic. "He's not going to wait for authorization from the shift commander. Do I pursue?"

Nick started to tell her about a shortcut.

"I know my way around Fossil Creek, Sergeant Matthews. I used to live here." She pressed the accelerator a bit harder, hoping slow and steady could win this race. "Which officer went into the bank?"

Her partner spoke into his cell phone. "What do we have at the bank? Any injuries?" He paused. "Hostages?" He shook his head.

Sarah kept driving, lights and siren blaring, but she wasn't going to be aggressive with a chase without orders. Not as a rookie. "The suspects aren't waiting around. Do we pursue?" she demanded. The orange car was speeding away, the sight sending adrenaline pumping through her veins. It rankled her to let a criminal get away.

The Chevelle was forcing motorists off the roads, amazingly, not causing any accidents. Its brake lights flashed like blinkers. From the sound of horns honking, the driver was obviously annoying locals stuck in five o'clock traffic.

Nick pulled the phone from his ear. "The suspects turned right on—" Before he could finish the sentence, Sarah cut over and turned off on a side street.

"We can catch up without fighting this heavy traffic."

He nodded and went back to his conversation with the shift supervisor.

Before she got any more response from Nick, dispatch came back with a report. The car had been stolen after a bank robbery in Omaha two days earlier.

"Stolen vehicle," Nick confirmed. "Follow, but take it easy. They're calling the commander."

"Three-eighteen in pursuit on Ram Ridge Road, southbound toward Horseshoe," Sarah told dispatch.

She waited for information from Nick, which didn't come. "Was someone hurt?" Depending on the answer, everything may have just changed.

"Yeah, are you comfortable with a high speed pursuit if necessary?" he asked. "We can call in someone else to intercept or set up a roadblock."

"This isn't my first pursuit, if that's what has you worried. And I have a perfect driving record."

"It was just an offer," he said, his deep voice tinged with sarcasm.

The car had turned back onto a main road, fighting traffic again, with Sarah on its tail. She watched drivers' reactions with dismay. One apparently didn't have good vision or hearing, for she didn't make any attempt to get out of the way. She should have noticed the flashing lights by now. Sarah hit the brakes and honked her horn. Finally, the driver swerved to the right, nearly hitting the cars that were already on the shoulder.

"Three-eighteen, status?" the dispatcher asked.

Nick responded before she could, leaving her free to focus on the pursuit. "We have the suspect in sight. The Chevelle is turning west on Horseshoe Loop." He leaned over and checked the speedometer. "Party is exceeding speed limits in heavy rush hour traffic."

"All officers in the vicinity west of Horseshoe and Dillon Road set up roadblock."

Oncoming traffic pulled to the shoulder, leaving Sarah an opening. She passed the remaining cars between her and the suspect, hitting a hundred miles an hour in seconds. The road turned from a four-lane to two, but traffic thinned considerably. "If I remember correctly, this road hooks left, then makes a quick right as it goes up the mountain toward the reservoir, correct?"

"Good memory."

"Think the driver knows that?"

"Yes on the road, no on suspects knowing the layout. You're doing great." Nick pressed one hand against the dash and spun the car-mounted laptop with the other so he could access the records on the suspects and the previous bank robbery.

"I'm going to…" Sarah started to say. As if their quarry realized they had no way out, they screeched to a halt, spun around and headed back toward the cruiser, black smoke billowing from the exhaust pipes.

"Aw, nuts!" she spat.

She hit the brakes and backed across the road, leaving her the option of going either direction. "Hang on!"

THREE

Nick couldn't believe the way Sarah handled the car, the chase and—if he were honest with himself—him. As the suspects raced closer, she stared them down, one hand on the wheel, one on the gearshift.

Once they'd left the city limits, Nick had alerted the sheriff's office that the chase was moving into their jurisdiction. Now, as they straddled the road, he heard another officer call in their exact location. "I haven't played chicken before, but this isn't looking good," Nick muttered.

"Show no fear," she whispered. Still focused on their quarry, she spoke with authority. "That car is souped up to the max. They aren't going to wreck it."

The suspects slowed almost to a stop as Roberts shimmied the cruiser forward, then back again when they attempted to get around it.

"They stole that vehicle," Nick reminded her.

She didn't bat an eye. "They could have stolen any number of cars in the Omaha area that would have garnered a lot less attention than an orange collectable car in pristine condition. They aren't going to damage it."

She said so with such confidence, he found it difficult to refute her reasoning. "And what makes you think that?"

She didn't answer.

Nick didn't wait. "So we can assume they're not from around here. That must be why they didn't want to go into the mountains on a two-lane road once you caught up to them."

"Don't you think they meant to turn toward the interstate and head for Denver?" she asked. She backed the cruiser up when they eased to the left, forward again when they tried once more to go around them to the right. "They don't know the area, they don't want to wreck the vehicle. They're up a creek without a paddle."

Nick jumped out of the cruiser and drew his gun. "Pop the trunk. I want to show them we mean business. Maybe they'll come to their senses." He made his way to the rear, his handgun zeroed in on the orange car's radiator.

"Careful," she said.

He lifted the trunk lid and pulled out both of their

rifles. "Lord, knock some sense into these two before we have to use our weapons." Backup had arrived, forming a line two deep behind the Chevelle. Sheriff's deputies came down off the mountain, forming a V-shaped blockade. The borrow ditches were ten feet deep, so the suspects weren't likely to take that route—in any car. They were blocked in totally, unless they used the vehicle as a ramming iron.

"Nick!"

He returned to the passenger's open door and handed Sarah a rifle. "Yeah?"

"The shift supervisor wants to talk to you."

"My hands are a little full right now. Can you put him on speakerphone?"

"Sure, Rambo," she teased.

Nick heard the phone beep as it switched to speaker mode. "Yeah?"

"These two are wanted in the murder of a security guard, injuring one of the bank tellers, and two officers in Nebraska. A car belonging to Ricky Turrow was found a block from where this car was stolen. Do what you have to, but we want to make sure it's the right guys. I've posted Turrow's mug shots from previous arrests on the system. Be careful, Matthews. The man has an ugly rap sheet."

"No kidding," Nick muttered. He leaned against

the squad car, trying to figure out what Turrow and his partner were planning.

Sarah pulled up the photo on the laptop screen. "It's Turrow."

Captain Thomas broke in to ask what was happening.

Nick raised his voice as he aimed his rifle. "For now, they're weighing their options—none of which are good. Any connection between the suspects and the owner of the car?"

"How'd you know?" the captain asked.

"It's Officer Roberts's belief that they have some attachment to it. They seem hesitant to take any risk of causing damage."

He heard a chuckle on the other end. "Welcome back, Matthews. See you soon." The cell phone went dead.

"Come out of the car, one at a time, and put your hands on your heads," he heard his trainee's authoritative voice bellow from the bullhorn under the hood of the car. "Driver first, Mr. Turrow."

Guns pointed at the car from every direction.

The orange Chevelle's engine revved and its tires squealed, sending smoke into the air again; obviously, the driver was racing the motor with his foot on the brake.

"You're not sitting in a very good position, Roberts," Nick warned. "Get out here."

"If they see a five-foot-one officer get out of the cruiser, they'll lose all fear, and you know it. Besides, someone needs to be ready in case they try to charge the barricade."

"No, you don't. Tell them we're going to shoot if they don't give up. I'll take out the tires, then the radiator, then the gas tank, in that order."

"What?"

"You heard me. Talk them out."

She cleared her throat, then got back on the bull-horn, speaking into the mike. "Give up, before someone else gets hurt."

The driver revved the engine again.

"Officers, prepare to open fire. On the three count, shoot out the tires!" she ordered over the mike.

The passenger waved his hand out the window. "Don't shoot the car! We give up!" He swore at his partner, obviously trying to convince him to surrender.

"Roberts, get out of the car," Nick said, as he inched around the cruiser and opened her door. "Hurry, while they're distracted." He kept his rifle aimed at the Chevelle's radiator. Someone was going to cry if he shot it, but it wouldn't be him. Roberts was his responsibility; he wasn't about to let her get hurt.

"Cut the engine and get out. I'm not calling them

off until you're both out of the car and on the ground," she bellowed as Nick tugged on her shirt-sleeve.

They could hear yelling from inside the car. Thirty seconds later, the driver turned off the Chevelle and gave himself up, followed by the passenger. Sarah burst out of the car, keeping her gun on the latter, Turrow, as Nick went to cuff and search the driver.

One of the sheriff's deputies nodded to her. "I think this is your arrest, Officer." He stood nearby as Sarah moved the suspect to the car to pat him down.

Nick wondered if he should turn his guy over to another deputy so he could help her. *Nope, she's just one of the guys; she's gotta do the job like all of us.* He glanced over, surprised that she didn't hesitate with any of her duties, even though the arrested party was a good foot taller than her.

"Get that cut on your forehead when you dived into the car?" she asked Turrow. "Take pictures," she said, motioning for another officer to snap some photos before she cuffed the man. "You're lucky that's all that happened to you, with your friend's driving habits, not to mention your bad choices," she added. "Keep your hands on the roof of the car."

Instead of obeying, the suspect threw an elbow into her chest, and again Nick fought the urge to intervene. The sheriff's deputy was there immediately to assist as needed. He kicked the suspect's legs farther apart.

"Is getting charged for resisting arrest and assaulting an officer part of your game plan?" Nick bellowed. He tightened his grip on his own suspect.

"C'mon, Turrow, you're not going anywhere, so how about acting like a gentleman?" Sarah said, trying to sweet-talk the guy into cuffs.

The man spit.

Stoically, Sarah pushed him against the car, finishing her search, removing a knife and two guns from the cargo pocket of his pants in the process. "You have the right to remain silent…."

He fidgeted, making it difficult to get the steel bracelets on him.

"These cuffs are too tight." The suspect jerked his arm from Sarah's grasp, then knocked her to the ground and started running.

FOUR

Nick shoved his prisoner into another officer's hands and headed toward Sarah.

She spun, kicking her suspect's legs out from under him. Then she jumped to her feet and put her knee between his shoulder blades. "Anything else you'd like to try?" she asked the guy laying with his face on the concrete. He had not only hers, but three other guns aimed at him.

Nick stopped on the other side of the prone figure, holding back a laugh. He waited as Sarah cuffed him, then helped her to pull the guy to his feet.

"Look what you did to me!" the bank robber said, blood dripping from his nose.

Sarah holstered her weapon and grabbed his arm. "I'd start exercising that right to remain silent if I were you." She escorted him to the backseat of their patrol car. "If you give up the right to remain silent, anything you say can and *will* be used against you in a court of law…." she said, then finished reading him his rights. She closed the door and looked at the prisoner sitting in a second cruiser. "Did you read your party his rights?" she asked Nick.

"Done. Unless you object, I'd like to send him ahead to the jail, put some space between these two so they can't collaborate on any details."

Officer Roberts jotted notes on a small pad. "Fine. We shouldn't be too long here, should we?"

"A tow truck has already been called to deliver the Chevelle to the police lot for investigation," Nick confirmed. "The officer who responded at the bank will meet us at the jail to help with questioning. The shift supervisor is contacting the Nebraska department to let them know we have their suspects."

"So we need to finish writing up our reports before they can be extradited to Omaha on their warrants."

"That's right. How's your report writing?" he asked.

"They're done differently than I'm used to, but I think I'm catching on." She looked up and smiled.

After the scene was cleaned up, they transported the prisoner to the jail and waited while the guards searched him and offered first aid. Since both suspects lawyered up, Nick and Sarah had to wait for legal counsel to arrive before they could question them.

"Good job out there, Officer Roberts," Nick said as they left the jail afterward.

"Thanks," she said, wondering if he was always so formal. She wanted to tell him to call her Sarah, but since he was her field training officer, she opted against saying anything. "I think it went amazingly well, considering no innocent victims were hurt and not one vehicle suffered any damage. I'm sure you have a few suggestions of how I could have handled it better…."

"I said you did a good job," Nick stated quietly.

She felt her heart beat a little faster when the corner of his mouth twitched. Sarah didn't dare let his compliment go to her head. Evaluation of a call was part of the job. She didn't need his approval. Or so she tried to convince herself.

A second later, he smiled. "Do you want to grab a soda on the way out, to celebrate?"

"Celebrate what? An arrest? Thanks, but I don't drink soda on duty."

"Coffee? Water? The machines have it all. My treat."

She finally gave in and turned down the hallway toward the lobby. "I need to call my sister real quick. If you insist on buying, I'll take a water."

She found a quiet corner and dialed her cell phone. "Hi, Beth. How're you doing?"

"Fine, until you called to remind me I shouldn't be," her baby sister mumbled. "I don't want to talk now."

Sarah paced the floor, knowing she'd feel much better if she was at home with her sister instead of counting on a bunch of uninformed friends to watch out for her. "Are your girlfriends there?"

"Yes. We're watching a movie and having pizza."

Sarah closed her eyes and took a deep breath. "You didn't let some pizza joint deliver to the house, did you? Did you even tell your friends what happened? Did you tell Steve yet?"

"I don't want to. I want to forget it," her sister said vehemently.

"That's not going to make it go away," Sarah warned in a hushed tone.

The line went dead as Beth hung up.

She felt a cold chill as a shadow made the corner go dark. "You okay?"

Sarah spun around, realizing Nick had returned with her bottle of water, and one for himself. "Yeah, you ready to go?" She hoped he didn't push for more information, because tonight, she didn't think she could stay quiet. She didn't want to be here at all, but she knew her sister's stubbornness would be as annoying in person as it was from a distance.

"I'm ready, if you're sure you are," he said skeptically. "Is your sister okay? You didn't sound very happy."

Sarah couldn't talk. Not right now. She walked past the good-looking officer who had been through the mill with his own problems. "I'm not."

"I don't mean to push…" he said under his breath. "But if you need time off, it's better to take it than try to carry on when you're distracted."

She stopped and turned to face him. "Did I seem distracted out there?"

He stepped back and crossed his arms in front of him, then dropped them to his sides, probably afraid he'd split the seams of his perfectly ironed shirt. "No."

"You probably know how irritating sisters can be when they make poor decisions, right?"

He looked at her, puzzled. "How'd you know I have a sister?"

Sarah couldn't believe she'd opened her big mouth. For some crazy reason, she'd hoped he would remember her. "We went to high school together." Suddenly she felt very awkward.

He didn't respond, but studied her. "She's not even close to our age. How'd…?"

"I saw her at basketball games." Sarah had done enough interrogation in her career to know that his pause was due to discomfort. She was just rankled enough from her conversation with Beth to push the topic. "You don't remember me, do you? I was older…. A geek with no social life…."

"I presume you still are," he said with an ornery smile. "Older, I mean."

She pursed her mouth and looked up at him. "Thanks for reminding me, Sergeant Matthews." She shrugged. "Forget I mentioned it. It's been a long time."

His lips quirked slightly, forming an adorable smile that she remembered from all those years ago. "I confess, I didn't make the connection at first. I thought you looked familiar. In this line of work, it's hard to remember where I've met someone. You're Joel's twin sister. I still can't believe you two are twins, he's so much taller…." Nick's face turned a shade pinker with her silence. "Sorry…."

She shook her head. "Yeah, thanks again for the reminder."

"He was a senior on the basketball team when I made varsity my sophomore year."

Sarah nodded in confirmation and his embarrassment faded. "And you bumped him out of the last quarter of the state championship game."

Nick shrugged, the blush returning with her statement. "Is the chip on his shoulder, or yours? That happened…" He paused thoughtfully "…fourteen years ago."

Sarah laughed at the puzzled look on his face.

"Oh, I think it bothered the rest of us a lot more than it ever did Joel. He was just happy that the team took the championship."

"We all were," Nick said as he opened the door to the parking yard. "For the record, you were a brainiac, not a geek. That's what everyone said, anyway." They continued out to the squad car in silence. Sarah's mind sped right back to high school, and the days she'd spent wishing she could be like the other girls for a change. The ones who were tall and pretty and knew how to flirt with boys, well enough to have gotten a date to the prom. Nothing scared high school boys away faster than a "brainiac," apparently.

So she'd reminded him. But was it a good thing that he remembered her, or bad?

She tore her mind from those days long ago and refocused on her sister. Sarah planned on making a slight detour by Beth's house, to make sure all was quiet.

"What's Joel doing now?"

Nick's question startled her. "Married with twin daughters, for starters. He teaches middle school in Denver."

"Sounds fun. And where's your sister?" he asked as they reached the cruiser and went to their respective doors.

At home, she hoped. Safe and sound. "She's here

in town." What was Beth thinking, giving out her name and address the day after someone assaulted her? Didn't she realize how fortunate it was that a group of students had happened by exactly when they did? Sarah got into the car and turned the key.

"Unlock my door," Nick called as he knocked on the passenger's window.

She hit the button, then offered a quick apology when he slid inside. "Well, that was a fun way to start the night, wasn't it?"

"Yeah," he said. "That ought to keep our blood pumping for a few hours, anyway." He asked a few more questions about Joel, but after that, it wasn't long before he became the strong silent type once again.

She wanted to keep him talking, but this being their first night of a four-week assignment, she decided to let him make conversation when he was comfortable doing so. She'd pushed enough for now.

Nick had a rough road ahead, regaining his footing in the department after the charges that had been made against him. She could sympathize. While her reasons for leaving the FBI were nowhere as difficult to handle emotionally as what he had been through, she still couldn't have walked back into the same team and pretended nothing had happened. In fact, she felt guilty leaving because they wouldn't let her work undercover assignments. In time, she was sure she'd have the chance to commiserate with him. For now, they needed to let the wounds heal.

Throughout the evening, they had little more than traffic stops to keep them awake. Finally, with an hour left in their shift, they returned to the station to complete their reports.

Nick barely said a word as he worked at the desk across from hers. She looked up once to find him staring at her.

"How's it going?" he said immediately.

He looked like the cat that had swallowed the canary. Sarah had the distinct feeling it wasn't reports that were on his mind. "Okay, I suppose. I'm not sure how to explain the cuts on Turrow's face."

"Self-defense. He was trying to escape."

She put her head in her hand. "There were four other officers between him and freedom. Would he really have run?"

"You bet. He was ready to take each officer out, and dumb enough to think he could get away with it." Nick walked around the desks and looked at what she'd written. "It happened faster than that. I barely took two steps before you'd taken him down. It was a natural reaction to a violent prisoner resisting arrest. Erase that sentence about your reasoning through it."

"But I did reason through it."

"You have ten years experience, Sarah." He said

her name with an edge of discomfort. "It's instinct to defend yourself and the other officers. You're trained to react to the opposition. Don't doubt yourself. That can't be any different on the streets than it was in the Bureau. There were enough officers around to verify that he'd elbowed you twice."

"You saw that?" Why had he been watching her, and not paying more attention to his own prisoner?

"You are my trainee. It's my responsibility to keep my eye on you," he said with a straight face.

So much for her high school dreams of a hometown boy finally noticing her, she thought. Sarah highlighted the sentence and hit the delete button, wishing it were as easy to erase her own mistakes.

FIVE

Nick reflected on his first night back on the job as he drove up the canyon west of town in the Colorado foothills. Officer Roberts wasn't far from his mind. It was difficult enough that his trainee was a former federal agent, but that it was brainiac Sarah Roberts made the assignment pure agony. Even though he knew it could be worse—he could be training a young rookie fresh out of the academy—he now regretted the day he'd accepted a field training officer assignment. That seemed a lifetime ago....

Before fellow officers had accused him of selling evidence to their drug ring.

Before his fiancée had walked off, worried that the scandal would ruin her journalism career.

Before his honor had been assaulted from every direction.

"I'm not sure how much more You think I can handle, God, but it might be time we have another discussion. Bringing an FBI agent to the department is one thing, but making my former high school crush my trainee is a really low blow."

As Nick pulled into the gravel driveway of the custom-built log home, his black Labrador greeted him from behind the six-foot chain link fence. She ambled toward the gate, her tail wagging and cheeks lifted in a smile. "Morning, Lexee."

She yipped a greeting, stretching her lanky body.

"You ready to go inside?" Though the dog had a door of her own into the garage, he opened the gate and brought her in through the main entrance with him.

The dog ran across the room, fetched a stuffed animal and attacked him with her toy. He couldn't help but smile. "You don't care what kind of night I had, do you?" he said as he tossed the toy down the hall for their early morning ritual. He filled a glass with orange juice and sat on the sofa to catch up with the news and baseball scores on his digital television recorder. The dog toy dropped at his feet and Lexee smiled at him again, eagerly awaiting the next toss. "You don't want to hear me complain about my cute new partner, do you?"

Lexee cocked her head to one side, as if to say, "Of course I do." Then she flung the toy at him and crouched, ready for him to throw it again.

The phone rang, and Nick jumped. He figured it

had to be one of his brothers calling to see how his first night back on patrol went. He checked the I.D. display to be sure it wasn't someone else calling at three in the morning.

"Hey, Garrett, what's up?"

"That's what I was going to ask you," his younger brother said. "I'm taking a break while it's quiet. Sounds like you had a fun evening. It's deader than a doornail now. Man, I'd have loved to have been in your boots!"

Nick smiled, thankful that he could share the peculiar sense of humor of the law enforcement officer with his family. What was bad to most people was great to a cop. "Yeah, it was a good evening. I suppose you also know that I finally made it as a field training officer," he said, waiting to see if his brother had heard that, too.

"Did you get the FBI agent?"

"Ten-four," he said with a chuckle. "What's worse, she went to high school here. I played basketball with her twin brother. We used to call her the brainiac. I guess I'm not done being investigated, after all."

"Get over that already, Nick. If they didn't trust you they would have come up with some reason to can you. I hear she whipped the bank robber. What's her name again?" his brother asked.

"Sarah Roberts. And yes, she has some pretty

amazing defensive moves. She's the shortest trainee with long dark hair…"

"Yeah," he said, obviously distracted. Nick could hear the radio in the background. "She didn't look familiar. Did I know her?"

Lexee dropped to her belly and squeaked the toy. Nick wrestled it away so he could hear Garrett, searching for something quieter to play with. "Probably not. Sarah and her twin brother are two years older than me, so she'd have been long gone by the time you and Kira were in high school. She remembered we'd adopted Kira."

"I think everyone remembers that. It was still pretty odd around here to see a mixed-race kid in our family."

"Yeah, I suppose so." Nick put his feet up and closed his eyes. "Her brother was the kid that I replaced in the championship basketball game my sophomore year. She razzed me about it. That was kind of weird." He didn't tell Garrett that she was even cuter now than she'd been in high school. "But all in all, it was a good night. It's definitely good to be back to work."

"And how'd the guys respond?"

Though Garrett couldn't see him, he shrugged. "About like we figured. Some were okay, but there were a lot who seemed sure I would kill their careers if they showed any support."

"At least you knew what to expect," Garrett conceded. "I thought you were imagining things until I saw guys avoiding me when they found out that we're related."

"I hate to say we told you so. I just can't help but wonder if they still suspect I was involved, and are trying to dig up some dirt. The captain either gave me the FTO to show his faith in me, or to let Sa... Roberts dig for more information." Nick cringed, hoping his brother didn't notice he'd almost called Sarah by her first name.

"Keep believing the first option, Nick. You have a good record on the force. Plus, it's only a few weeks. It won't take long for things to return to normal."

Nick gave a quick overview of the bank robber call, hoping Garrett would overlook his slip. "Has anything new been mentioned about the assault victim?"

"Yeah, didn't you hear rumors that the mayor is raising a ruckus over it? This is the second woman assaulted in the last five months. The last victim was leaving a church meeting...."

"And who would tell me the latest rumblings from City Hall? It's not like Kent hears the downtown rumors from the undercover narcotics office."

"Are you kidding? Half the time they're the first to know. It's like they have a bug in the locker room sometimes." His younger brother hesitated. "Well, rumor has it we may all be assigned partners until this rapist is caught."

Lexee dropped the toy and Nick snatched it away. She jumped for it as he tucked it behind his back. He tossed the dog a tennis ball, hoping it would keep her busier than the squeaky stuffed animal.

"You haven't heard a name yet? No suspects?" he asked.

"We've just been told to keep a close eye on the university, so I presume she was a student or an employee there. Why?"

"I don't know. It seemed kind of odd that Roberts didn't mention it. I mean, everyone in the men's locker room was discussing it. Roberts and I were right there on the east side of campus, and she never said a word about it."

The line was quiet for a minute before his brother responded. "She was probably overwhelmed from the bank robbery. I'm guessing that's her first really good incident on street duty. Give it some time. She'll be talking your ear off as soon as she gets comfortable."

Nick didn't dare admit that he was probably as hyped up about the robbery as she was. She'd been one hundred percent in control of the situation. Completely sure of her every move, which made her that much more dangerous as a trainee.

He'd have to make sure she didn't push too far.

Take too many liberties. Do any damage to his already tenuous reputation.

"Nick?" His brother's voice broke into his thoughts.

"Yeah. I should let you get back to work. I need to go in early to order some new uniform shirts. Seems I gained a little weight in the last three years in plainclothes."

"Maybe you should reconsider playing basketball with the police team this winter. I'll work it off of you," Garrett said with a chuckle.

"I'm sure nothing would make you happier than to do it, either."

Nick set the phone back on the charger and locked up the house.

Instead of falling asleep like he usually did right after coming home, he found himself wide awake thinking of Sarah Roberts. He pulled his high school yearbook off the shelf and thumbed through the slick pages, admiring a much younger version of his partner.

She wore her hair down in those days with bangs hanging into her eyes. He remembered it as if it were just yesterday. He'd been too shy then to talk to her let alone ask a senior girl out.

He couldn't help but wonder what would have happened if he had?

SIX

Sarah had checked in with her sister every day since the attack. Pretending everything was okay seemed to be catching up with her; Beth hadn't attended her night class all week. At some point, Sarah had to convince her it was time she get professional help.

Sarah called after work one night, only to be greeted by a very grouchy voice. "I'm fine. I was sound asleep," Beth mumbled.

"I'm sorry, I figured you'd still be awake, like usual. It's only two-thirty in the morning."

Her sister yawned. "I'm turning over a new leaf, getting to bed when normal people do."

It sounded like depression to Sarah. "I just wanted to talk to you about seeing a counselor, Beth."

"Sarah! Drop the subject. You're only making things worse."

Beth refused to deal with this. She wouldn't tell their parents, though Sarah didn't totally blame her there; they'd be on the next plane to Colorado. "Beth, it's not just going to go away."

"Don't…" Her voice cracked. "Sarah, don't start…. Go home and get some sleep."

"Later then," she said gently.

The line went dead, and Sarah stared at her sister's darkened windows. For now, all she could do to protect her was to check to make sure the doors were locked and no one was lurking outside.

Sarah went home to her apartment and went to bed, but no matter how much warm milk she drank, or how many pages of her book she tried to read, she wasn't sleepy. She struggled to follow her sister's wishes to leave her alone. Unfortunately, that was easier said than done. She'd grown up protecting her siblings. As the oldest, even if only by ten minutes, she felt it was her self-appointed duty.

After traveling the world as a military brat, she'd gone to college planning to teach foreign languages. When one of her roommates was raped in the bedroom across the hall, however, Sarah changed her major to criminal justice and found her niche, even if it had taken awhile to figure out exactly what aspect of law enforcement fit her the best.

How could Beth, the free-spirited youngest child, expect Sarah to turn off her concern? It was time she shared what had happened to her roommate. She needed Beth to realize she wasn't just being a cop, she was a sister, too.

After three hours in bed, tossing and turning, Sarah gave up trying to sleep. She unpacked a few boxes, went shopping for some fall decorations and stopped in to get her hair trimmed. She tried everything she could to avoid thinking about her sister and her new training officer. Doing so was pointless. She needed to ease her mind about Beth so she could focus on her job.

Her sister had ignored her phone calls for two days, leaving messages when she knew Sarah couldn't answer. Sarah couldn't stand it anymore; she went to Beth's house, only to find she wasn't home.

Sarah waited outside the small two-story until it was time to go to work. After four days of the swing shift, worrying about her sister, and trying to gain the trust of her untrusting training officer, Sarah just wanted to be there to help Beth cope with the after-effects of the assault. She was the only person her sister had confided in, and that, too, was a burden she didn't take lightly.

She hurried into the police station with just enough time to get dressed and duck into the briefing. She wasn't ready for another night of strained silence with Nick Matthews. Every time she opened her mouth she was afraid she'd say something stupid about the crush she'd had on him in school. That he'd thought of her as a brain wouldn't be half-bad, if he hadn't added "iac" to the end of it. That said it all. He'd thought of her as a nerd. He was trying to be nice.

The other female officers had left the locker room when she heard the door open. Nick Matthews called her name.

"Yeah?" she said, fastening her Kevlar vest over a black T-shirt.

"Hustle, would you? We need to get over to the jail and question our bank robbers. Their lawyers just got here and don't have any patience. It's okay they kept us waiting five days to question our defendants, but they can't wait ten minutes."

She slipped her uniform shirt on, doing up the bottom few buttons so she could tuck it in and fasten her pants. She tugged her tactical boots onto her feet, dropped her hair clips into her breast pocket and stuffed her street clothes into her locker. She was out the door two minutes later, wrapping her loaded equipment belt around her waist as she met Sergeant Matthews in the hall. She'd laced up her boots so she didn't stumble, but saved the rest of her primping, not wanting to keep him waiting.

He took one glance at her and raised an eyebrow,

erasing an ambiguous smile from his lips. "You don't plan to go into the men's jail looking like that, do you?" He flicked her hair from her shoulder.

She held up her hand, showing him the hair band around her wrist. "You said hustle—I'm here." Sarah combed her hair into a braid with her fingers and pulled a hair clip from her pocket. She normally fixed her hair ·at home, but with her concern for Beth, nothing had gone as planned.

"One demerit for sloppy uniform, two extra points for hustling. You might want to finish buttoning up, Officer Roberts. I'll drive."

Sarah took two steps to his one, feeling tiny next to him. She hurried to button her shirt before they reached the car. "So why are these lawyers in such a big rush?"

"Probably so they can go out for dinner. Who wants to sit with a couple of convicts when they could be out on the town?"

Sarah groaned. This wasn't a good way to start the night. She hadn't slept well, worrying about how to get her sister to come to her senses. When she'd applied for this job, she had never thought about how difficult it would be to leave a case that involved her own family for someone else to handle. And she knew that when her parents found out Beth hadn't told them right away, they'd hit the ceiling. It had already been a week since the assault.

They finished the interviews with Turrow and his getaway driver and headed out on patrol. She didn't think it possible, but Nick was even quieter than he had been the other nights. If it hadn't been for one boring call after another, they'd have had no communication at all.

Just as they walked into a burger joint for a quick bite, another call came in. "All units to the university. Backup assistance requested at an on-campus disturbance." At least the call gave them a break from the confines of the car, where the dispatcher's voice almost became welcome company.

Nick was the first to turn around and head back to the squad car. "What's another hour without food," he said to Sarah as she followed. "Officer 318 responding with FTO 235. Cancel our dinner break."

"Copy 235 and 318. Better luck next time," the dispatcher said, a hint of sympathy in her voice. She gave the address of the disturbance as Sarah pulled out of the parking lot onto University Drive.

When they arrived, teens and young adults littered the lawn of the huge, two-story, gothic-style house.

"You can always tell when it's rush week," Sarah muttered to Nick as she turned on the police lights and pulled to a stop in the street. They climbed out of the squad car and approached the campus police chief. "I'm Officer Roberts and this is my FTO, Sergeant Matthews. How do you want us to help?"

"We're trying to get everyone inside, first off. We cite for underage consumption. If we have any minors, ticket them, and contact the parents. Watch for dangerous levels of intoxication and alcohol poisoning. We have an ambulance on standby, just in case. Check every room and closet. I don't want another surprise, like the death we had last year. Didn't you work that investigation, Matthews?"

"I did." Nick quickly told Sarah about the girl who'd passed out in a closet, to be found dead several days later.

Officers were corralling people and ushering them back inside. As she contacted the students, Sarah struggled with the realization that the man who'd attacked her sister could be nearby, watching, selecting his next victim. She leaned over to look at a young man Nick was cuffing. No match to her sister's description. The only similarity was his dark hair.

You can't get involved, Sarah. Leave it to the detective assigned to her case.

Nick looked at her strangely, glanced around the crowd, then to his suspect. "What?"

"I was thinking about that APB from the other night," she whispered. "I thought he looked a little like the suspect."

Nick looked at the kid, then back to her. "Stick close, in case you have questions."

Sarah was stunned by his remark, but tried to convince herself that he was under a lot of stress, too, and probably didn't mean that the way it came out. She wasn't a rookie in the traditional sense of the word, but she had to remember that that didn't remove any responsibility from his shoulders.

She had to get past her insecurities all over again, only it was worse this time. Before, she'd been a five foot one, twenty-four-year-old woman fighting for respect among the elite agents of the FBI, with all their expectations. For some idiotic reason, she hadn't thought she'd have to prove her competency now, after ten years experience. The first time she had every reason to feel insecure. This time she had no excuse. She was her own worst enemy.

She shook her head and put her mind back on the task at hand—catching underage drinkers; keeping the public safe and drunk drivers off the streets. She'd come home to reach out to the community. That was why she left the FBI—to have a chance to make a difference. This was where she needed to be. She was sure of it.

Once they'd gotten everyone inside, officers were posted at the doors while everything was sorted out, closets checked and alcohol levels measured.

"Your driver's license or identification, please," Sarah asked a woman who looked far too young to be at a college party.

"I'm not drunk," she snapped.

Since Sarah hadn't mentioned alcohol or any other accusation, the girl's defiance sounded like a blatant confession. "Good, then you won't mind breathing into this…." Sarah handed her a Breathalyzer, fighting the urge to inform her of what could have happened from being so careless. She thought of what had happened to her sister the week before, without being under the influence of alcohol. These kids didn't want to face facts, and while Sarah remembered those days, she wished she could make a difference.

"No way," the girl said, pushing Sarah's hand away.

"If you choose not to provide your I.D. or take the breath test, we'll need to take you to the police department for questioning."

Nick moved closer, as if concerned about how she was handling the situation.

"I'm not drunk," the young woman repeated, sticking her nose in the air.

Sarah noted the fear in her eyes and thought of her sister. "You're making this worse than it needs to be," she said softly. "Right now, I suspect there's an underage drinking citation to issue, but we're here to help maintain safety for everyone. Alcohol consumption could impair your judgment, make you more vulnerable…." Sarah looked her in the eye, noting tears forming. She imagined Beth, and the many times she'd gotten into trouble merely by refusing to think anyone would spike a drink, drive drunk or intentionally harm her, and Sarah's heart softened. Kids make mistakes, she reminded herself. She'd even made a few herself. "We're not trying to make your life miserable. What's your name?"

The tears streamed down her face. She wrapped her arms around her body. "Tiffany... I need to go home." The young woman trembled.

"Not yet, Tiffany. Tell us what you know about who is hosting."

"I don't know," she answered. "A friend invited me to come with her. She'd heard about this huge party on the Internet. I only had one drink," Tiffany said, holding up a plastic cup.

Sarah was puzzled. "Help me understand. Your friend got an e-mailed invitation, but didn't tell you who was hosting?"

"It wasn't an e-mail, it was on an announcement board."

Sarah guessed the girl to be about nineteen, maybe twenty at the most. Too old to be so naive. "And you never questioned whether it might be safe?"

She shrugged. "No."

Sarah couldn't believe that with all the education on personal and online safety, this was still happening.

"So was it a campus announcement board?"

"No, it was…" she closed her eyes and swayed a little "…an online announcement board," she repeated, obviously growing more irritated with Sarah's questions.

"Where did you say the invitation was posted?"

"I didn't."

"It would help us keep campus safe if we knew."

The young woman rolled her eyes. "I'm not sure, but probably on Coedspace," she muttered. "Now can I go?" she asked defiantly. Her eyes wandered, not tracking well. "I've got to go."

"Are you okay?" Sarah stepped back, in case the girl got sick. What she had done to finally get through to her, Sarah wasn't sure, but she was relieved that they had made progress. "Why don't I take that cup for you?" Sarah reached out, but Tiffany didn't respond, just swayed. "What's your last name and address, Tiffany?"

"Tiffany…" she said as she collapsed.

Nick stepped up, catching her before she hit the ground. Sarah called for the ambulance, picked up the plastic cup and shoved the other students away.

High-pitched voices screamed all around them, like the wave at an athletic event.

Nick carried the girl outside as Sarah cleared a path so the paramedics could pull the gurney up and examine her. "Did you catch her name?" he asked.

"Just Tiffany." Sarah asked the medic for a bag for the cup. Maybe they'd be able to get an analysis of the contents. "She insisted she had only one beer, and she saw the kid pour it from a bottle. She claimed this was her cup." She told the paramedics about the girl swaying and clutching her stomach as she'd interviewed her.

Nick shook his head as they walked back inside. "Don't these kids realize how easily bottles can be tainted, then recapped? Or drinks doctored? I mean, why else pour them into a cup?"

"Tiffany!" a young woman screamed, bolting past the officer guarding the door.

Nick stopped her. "You know Tiffany?"

"We're roommates," she cried. "Is she okay? What happened?"

"We don't know yet. She collapsed. We need to get some information from you so we can contact her family," Sarah said, hoping to get Tiffany's personal details from the roommate. When she had done so, Nick questioned the woman further about the party, while Sarah took the information to the paramedics, who were stabilizing their patient before transporting her to the hospital.

Sarah rejoined Nick after the ambulance left. Two hours later, they finally finished policing the party—weeding out underage drinkers, sending those who were sober back to their dorm rooms with campus security officers, and transporting half a dozen more who were dangerously intoxicated to the hospital. The renters of the house, however, were nowhere to be found.

The place was tucked among a full block of fraternity and sorority houses less than two miles from Beth's home. No one present tonight had seemed to know if this particular house was one of them, or just an unofficial place to party without putting any group's charter in jeopardy.

After they finished there, Nick and Sarah stopped at the hospital to check up on Tiffany. She had definitely been slipped something, but the drug hadn't been identified yet. She was going to be okay—for today.

When they got back to the precinct, Sarah logged on to the computer. She found just how easy it was to get to the message boards after creating a user name.

"Nick, look at this," she said. "It's the announcement for the party. It doesn't even give a name for who's hosting, just an address."

He leaned over her shoulder to read the invitation. A few seconds later, he pressed the print icon, making an electronic image of the post, then suggested she send it to the campus police chief and their detectives. "Maybe between them they can find out who posted the message."

Sarah opened her e-mail and sent the link to both of the men Nick had suggested. "Does the Fossil Creek PD ever offer community safety workshops? I think this is something we need to make public."

"I agree. I know this is a campus issue, but it pertains to everyone in the community." Nick leaned closer. "It looks like there are also faculty and staff from the college on here." He pointed to a name. "Is that a relative of yours?"

Sarah's eyes widened and her heart raced. "It's my sister."

SEVEN

Sarah clicked on Beth Roberts's profile as Nick looked over her shoulder. "Is that correct?" he asked as he pointed to the home address space.

She didn't answer.

"She obviously isn't worried about someone finding her. You might want to remind her that with you working in town now—"

"I've already tried," Sarah said, frustration spewing from her like lava from a volcano. "Believe me, I've tried."

He noted the suddenly ashen color of her face. "Is there anything I can do?"

She closed the Web site and logged off the computer. "If you have any changes you want me to make on the reports, let me know. I need to go talk to my sister. Again."

A few minutes later, Sarah rushed out of the women's locker room, dressed in her street clothes, and headed toward the exit. Nick stopped her. "We need to talk, Officer Roberts."

"It's a family matter and has nothing to do with the…this case…Sergeant."

He wanted more than anything to believe her. But there was fear in her dark brown eyes, as well as fury. "What *does* it have to do with then?"

Sarah looked around uncomfortably, slipping her arms into the sleeves of her fitted jacket. "My sister's…safety. I can't talk about it. I need to go."

"Why *not* talk about it?" He motioned to their surroundings. "Not here, you mean? Not to me? What's wrong?"

"Not here, not with you." She looked him in the eye and he knew something was really wrong. "Trust me, you don't need to know."

Nick felt the knife in his back again. Except this petite woman was standing right in front of him, and had more power to bring him down than a Mack truck.

He took a calming breath. This wasn't the two fellow cops he'd trusted evidence to; she was asking him to let her handle her sister.

Like he and his brother had stepped in to help their sister just a few months earlier. "I've been down this road already, Officer. I'm your FTO and you're leaving before finishing reports. I'd say I need to know," he argued. "You may have credentials to get you here, but it's my duty to make sure you know how to survive. And I can assure you, a distracted officer may as well be going in front of a firing line without body armor."

The silence between them lengthened as footsteps echoed down the hall. Sarah's voice softened as she said, "I wouldn't do that to you." She glanced up, pleading with him. "Never."

What was that supposed to mean? Did she know what he'd been through? Was she testing him? What could he say? "It's nothing personal, Officer Roberts. I don't trust anyone anymore. I've been blindsided once, but I learned my lesson. So your sister innocently put her address on the Web. Almost everyone's information can be found on the Internet if you look hard enough."

"I know that all too well." She nodded. "But I've been trying to reach Beth for hours. She's not answering. I went by her house before our shift, and she wasn't there."

"You typically check in on her more than once a day?" He crossed his arms over his chest and waited. There had to be more to the story than an overly protective sister. "Is there something wrong with her? I mean, sorry, Roberts, but you're sounding a little—"

She held up her hand to stop him. "Don't go there, Nick." As if she realized she'd just called him by his first name again, she shook her head and looked at him. "Sergeant Matthews, pardon me. But don't even—" Her voice cracked. "I've got to go."

"I didn't mean to upset you, Sarah." He waited for her to question his own lack of protocol. "We're clearly off duty now."

She nodded. "Let's take it outside then."

Nick followed her as she moved toward the door. "I think you'd better tell me what's going on."

She stopped and stared at him as if they were a couple of teenagers playing games. "I told you the truth. This isn't because of the case. I need to talk to my sister, as a sister, not as a police officer."

"Your car or mine then?" he suggested.

He wasn't going to give in. "Fine, I'll meet you in an hour at a restaurant. Just tell me where." She looked down at her purse and dug for her keys.

"No way. If you're not going to talk about it here in private, you think I believe you'll tell me what's going on in a public restaurant? Until I find out what this is about, I'm your shadow."

She pulled the tie from her braid, unraveled her hair and tossed the thick waves over her shoulders. He recalled how soft it had felt when he'd touched it before their shift began.

"Fine, follow me to my sister's house. I'll show you. All I need to do is make sure she's okay."

"I've seen your driving skills. I'm not going to try to keep up. So, do you want to drive, or shall I?"

"I will," she conceded, heading out the door.

Nick followed, hoping he didn't regret pushing her so hard. He removed his uniform shirt and Kevlar vest, leaving just the sweaty under-armor shirt. He tossed the garments onto the floor of her sport utility vehicle as he got inside. "So what's going on?"

Sarah remained silent, backing out of the parking space quickly. "My sister isn't answering my phone calls. She had a confrontation after class the other night. I'm worried."

"I got that. So what about the confrontation makes you think she's in danger?"

"She didn't know the guy, or have any idea why he'd been waiting outside the classroom for her."

Sarah didn't say as much, but the clues were all there. Nick was beginning to despise the accuracy of his gut instinct. How could he tell her that he'd suspected she had some personal connection to the assault case? Everyone, all the male officers, had been talking about it at the station. It made no sense that she hadn't been. "I'm sorry, Sarah."

"Me, too, since she lives alone in a little house right off campus. She hasn't returned my calls in days. Yesterday, she wasn't home. Now I find her street address on a college community Web site? How can someone with a master's degree be so naive?" With each sentence, his partner seemed more and more relieved to be able to share her concerns.

Nick remembered all the turmoil stirred up by his own problems. "I don't know your sister, but I really do understand how you're feeling." Would he be opening himself up to more pain by sharing his own mistakes? Or did she already know? "As your FTO, I have to remind you to stay out of any active investigation. Is there one?"

She came to a stop at a red light and turned to him. "I don't need a training officer right now, Nick. I'm not investigating, I'm checking on my sister."

"Because of information you found that you think links her to a crime. I shouldn't have to tell you, that's a pretty fine line."

"I can understand why you're suspicious, but I'm not here to test you. I am separated from the FBI, forever. I'm the one at *your* mercy right now, and believe me, I wish you weren't here."

He gave her a critical stare.

"Right now, I'm a big sister." She held out her hands. "Look, no uniform, no badge. I'm a civilian. If you're going to search me, my gun's in my bag." She stared at him.

"You're blowing my concern all out of proportion, Sarah."

"Even if I do seem like a bossy big sister, I'm sorry, that's who I am. So if you have a problem with that, get out now." The light changed, but Sarah didn't move. "Does that mean you're okay with this?"

"It's green and you're blocking traffic. Get going," he said impatiently. He understood her position, but after being stabbed in the back, he wanted to avoid any questionable calls.

She drove on through the intersection, not giving him another chance to climb out.

"You're going to talk to your sister. Nothing wrong with that." He didn't dare tell Sarah he was concerned about her, too. He shouldn't be, he knew; he'd seen firsthand that she could take care of herself. Still, he didn't understand this need he had to find out more about her and her obsession to take care of her sister. He didn't like the fact that he wanted to get involved. "As soon as you confirm she's okay, call the detective, leave him a message about what you've found, and walk away."

"But if something *is* wrong, I'm not walking," she said as she swiftly turned the next corner.

"If it means a conviction or not, you will, on your own or by force. I'll handle it if necessary." What was he saying? Why would he put himself on the line for a trainee, after officers he'd known for years had betrayed him?

"If something's wrong, you call dispatch and get lost," she countered. "I'm not going to put *your* career in jeopardy, Nick. You shouldn't even be here now."

"If your sister was involved in a case, *you'd* better get lost…." They tossed warnings back and forth like a hot potato, but when it came right down to it, he knew it wasn't in the nature of either of them to walk away. If something had happened, they'd both be right in the middle of it to the very end.

And that scared him to death. How could he have jumped right into another mess when he was being so careful to hold the world at arm's length?

"You're not even out of training yet. You can't start stepping on toes."

A smile teased Sarah's lips. "Like you'll let me after that? I'll look forward to accepting that offer one day, Sergeant." Suddenly the tension broke, as Nick realized that was not a professional response.

He didn't dare answer. Yeah, she was cute, and feisty, and just the kind of woman he could probably relate to, but she was his trainee. That was a flashing red light if he'd ever seen one.

Imminent danger.

Pulling away from the next stop sign, Sarah did what he should have long ago. Changed the subject. "It's pretty clear that everyone thinks I'm working for Internal Affairs. They don't trust me, and you don't, either." She waited, as if he'd missed a question in her statement.

Nick shook off the realization that he'd like to accept her challenge. He forced her last comment to replay in his mind. "I don't trust anyone anymore. Don't take it personally. Only my brothers, and thanks to my careless mistake, no one trusts them now, either."

"That's a pretty heavy burden to carry."

"Apparently this issue with your sister is, too. You going to tell me what happened?"

She shook her head. "First, I need to make sure she's okay. She doesn't want to believe—"

As Sarah turned the corner, they both saw the flashing red and blue lights of three police cars ahead. She stopped right there in the middle of the road.

"Sarah, what…why are you stopping?"

"That's my sister's house!"

EIGHT

Sarah froze.

"Pull over," Nick was telling her. "I think you'd better give me a little more to go on when I approach the officers with questions. You sure she didn't know the guy who confronted her? Just how far did this confrontation go?"

"I can't…"

"I'm your training officer. You'd better rethink your evaluation of 'can't,' because I *can't* be here with you off duty without a very good explanation. So you'd better make it good. Now."

Sarah slapped the palm of her hand against the steering wheel. She'd promised herself she wouldn't get involved in the investigation. She'd promised Nick she wouldn't hurt him, and that was a promise she had every intention of keeping. "My sister was the most recent assault victim," she said in a whisper.

Nick didn't say anything, but she'd been around

enough officers to have a pretty good guess what he was wishing he could say.

She hated the silence. The not knowing. Not being able to dig for answers. "What if he found where she lives? What if that's why the police are here?"

Without answering, Nick opened the door and got out. "Don't you dare keep something that critical from me again. You wait here," he growled, "And I mean don't get out of this car until I say so!" He slammed the door and jogged ahead to question their fellow officers.

She couldn't believe this was happening—again. She wanted nothing more than to just back off and let the officers do their jobs.

What was it about her that couldn't walk away and let someone else be in charge? Sarah hadn't meant to get involved with her sister's case. Why was it always she who exposed the missing link in her superiors' cases?

Something in her gut told her she had happened upon information now that could change the course of the investigation, but how was she going to trust that information to anyone else?

The online community might not have anything to do with Beth's assault, she mentally argued. Out of thirty thousand students on campus, less than a tenth of them had listings on the Coedspace Web site.

On the other hand, finding Beth's name on Co-edspace might be the break that they needed....

What would Sarah do if he'd found her sister again?

God, how could You let this happen to Beth? Why?

Sarah hadn't talked to God in years, and it probably wasn't a great way to get back in His good graces to challenge His authority. Still, Beth had devoted her life to Him. Where was He when she'd needed Him most?

Sarah had tried her sister's cell phone so many times, she wondered if she needed to refresh the phone's memory. She entered the number again, hoping this time Beth would answer.

Sarah couldn't believe something else had happened. Criminals weren't generally the brightest candles in the box, but it wasn't uncommon for them to come back to watch their crime be discovered. She looked around, hoping he'd returned, though attacking at the victim's home wasn't this perp's pattern.

Maybe it was a copycatter? Or just a coincidence? Gangs had been tagging their territories lately.

Blood pulsed through her temples.

Sarah hit the send button again. Tired of leaving the same frantic message, she simply hung up when the voice mail message started.

Or was this suspect really targeting specific women?

She thought back to the last time she and Beth had talked. It had been two days since Sarah had reached her, not a machine, and about a day since she'd received a message back. Long enough to file a missing person report...

Sarah wanted to believe this was simply a case of a stubborn sister trying to assert her independence, not that Beth was in danger. The flashing lights ahead of her said otherwise.

She watched Nick talk to the officer on duty. Eyeing his uniform shirt and Kevlar vest at her feet, she found her mind wandering to his situation. He was one of the best-looking eligible bachelors on the force. She couldn't believe some woman hadn't caught him yet....

Sarah wondered if her sister had a key to the house hidden anywhere. She pressed Send again, trying to pull her attention away from her forbidden attraction.

No answer.

Nick turned and looked in her direction, then disappeared into the alley next to Beth's house.

That wasn't good. What was in the alley?

Please don't let it be Beth. Please, God, take care of my little sister.

Sarah dialed again, hoping it wouldn't be one of

the officers who answered. The call immediately went to voice mail.

The next one she made had to be to her parents. She had to let them know something was wrong.

She half expected an ambulance to pull up at any moment. If they'd found her sister…

Nick reappeared out of the shadows of the night and shook his head, then started walking toward her.

From the look on his face, she could tell he wasn't bearing good news. He walked up to her door, not his own. Another bad sign.

"They need to talk to you."

She shook her head. "What is it?" It was nearly two in the morning and this wasn't the kind of adrenaline rush she was used to. She hadn't been to sleep in almost twenty hours. Her body wanted to shut down, but her brain wasn't about to let her. Not until she found her sister. She felt nauseous. "Nick? What's happened?"

"Park the car, and I'll go with you."

She did so and jumped out. "What happened? Tell me!"

"A car's been vandalized." He stepped closer and put his hand on her shoulder.

"The car? You're going through all this over her car? I don't think so. What really happened? Is it Beth?"

"They got a call reporting a barking dog and gunshots. When the police arrived, they found…signs of a struggle…. The crime scene investigations unit is on their way, to determine whether it's even human blood. Does your sister or one of her neighbors have a dog?"

Sarah shrugged, noting her shoulder didn't move much since she was tucked tightly against Nick. "Beth doesn't, and I don't remember whether a neighbor did or not." She stopped and looked into his eyes, searching for the truth. "Just tell me, so I can be prepared. Is there a body?"

"No," he said. "That's the good news. Which is better than the bad news, isn't it? They need you to see if the car out back of the house is your sister's."

Suddenly her mind went blank, and she found it difficult to breathe, let alone walk. "They can't identify it by the license plates?"

"No, they're gone." Nick looked into her eyes, and she could see his fear. Feel his sympathy. "Do you have a key to your sister's house?"

She shook her head. "Not anymore, and she's still not answering her phone. But you didn't hear a phone ring, right?"

He took hold of her shoulders. "No, we didn't hear a phone. But don't panic, Sarah. We're going to get to the bottom of this."

"What if someone took—"

"Don't assume anything, Sarah," Nick said

gently. "I know how tough that is right now, but we have to pray that she's okay." He patted her shoulder and gave her a tender hug.

Sarah swallowed hard, willing back the tears she wanted so badly to shed.

Nick led her to the officer in the alley. He'd been one of the instructors during her classroom training.

"Hi, Sarah," Jeremy said. "We just missed you at the precinct, I guess. They said you'd left. We got a call for gunshots and a barking dog at 1:37 a.m. Apparently dispatch put a watch on your sister's address after a report a few days ago. We haven't gotten details on that call yet."

"You won't," Sarah said, suddenly missing the security of Nick's embrace. How had she not noticed when he'd slipped his arm away? She shivered now as she looked at the vehicle.

The car had a broken side window, scratched paint and a side mirror hanging by a wire. The tires had been slashed. This was not her sister's car. Was it? "It's a…confidential case," she said, trying to put out of her mind that this was a personal issue, too.

She needed to turn off the emotions, keep her cool. She took a deep breath. Then another. "I found out tonight that she listed her real address at an online community, so this might be related."

"We need you to verify if it's her vehicle…." The officer shone his flashlight on the economy car.

Sarah covered her mouth with her fingers as she studied it. The sedan was pale blue like Beth's, but something was wrong….

When she stepped closer, Nick put his hand out to stop her. "It's evidence…."

"Blood, you mean. I do know how to approach a crime scene, Sergeant." She motioned for a flashlight, and Jeremy Logan handed it over without a word. Maintaining a wide berth, Sarah walked around the car and looked into the backseat.

Placing some distance between herself and her training officer probably wasn't a bad idea, either.

"It's different when it may involve family," he said gently as she walked past him. "Is it your sister's?"

"It looks just like it, but she had a stuffed animal in the back window. A lamb. It was her reminder that God went wherever she went."

"We found a stuffed animal a few feet down the alley. It looks like someone or something was dragged out of here. Officer Matthews is following the trail. Garrett…Nick's brother."

Sarah shook her head. "And we have no idea if it was my sister…." The men were looking at her as if she might faint at any moment.

"When was the last time you talked to your sister?" Jeremy asked.

"I spoke to her on the phone about forty-nine

hours ago. She left a message at one-thirty yester-day morning, when I was writing reports."

"That's pretty precise," he said suspiciously.

"I just calculated how long it had been as I was waiting in the car. I was trying to figure out if it's been long enough to file a missing person report."

Sergeant Logan looked at her, puzzled. "And did you?"

"No. Not yet. After her incident, Beth didn't want to talk or think about it. I was the only person whom she'd told, so I brought back those memories to her, I guess. I wanted to give her space, but I…" She looked at the car again, then took a deep breath. "I shouldn't have pushed her so hard to talk about it. I pushed her away. I went by her house about eight yesterday morning to try to talk to her, but she wasn't home. She hasn't answered any of my phone calls all day today. I checked her house before my shift, and she wasn't in."

"Is that unusual for your sister?" Sergeant Logan asked. "To just go away without…"

Sarah nodded. "She normally tells me if she goes anywhere for any length of time. I moved here to be closer to my sister and brother. Until I went to Washington to work with the FBI, we were all very close."

"We tried ringing her doorbell, but no one answered. Do you have a key so we can make sure the house is okay?"

"No, but I'm good at picking locks. Unless you'd rather…" she said, looking at Jeremy.

He handed her his pick set. "Be my guest. And where are your parents? Could she have gone to see them? Have they talked to her today?"

The three of them walked up to the house. "No, they're in Montana." Sarah made quick work of unlocking the door, as Jeremy held the flashlight. "I don't know if they have talked to her."

After a rapid inspection revealed no one was home, Sarah glanced over to Nick as she left the house for the officers to investigate. "I guess it's time I call them, see if they can reach her. Beth didn't want them to know what happened, but I can't keep it quiet any longer. I can't get her to call me, and now her voice mail is full, I guess. It's not even picking up anymore."

"Give me her number. I'll try to reach her," Nick said.

"No," Sarah said hesitantly. "If she hears an unfamiliar man's voice, it may freak her out, and she won't call back. Let me try my mom and dad first." She pulled out her cell phone from the belt clip and dialed, wondering how she could explain calling at three-thirty in the morning, a week after the incident. She didn't want to worry them, but it was well past time to worry, in her estimation.

She couldn't deal with this alone. She'd crumble

for sure. She'd already made a mess of her job, her relationship with her training officer. She'd probably already killed her career hopes.

She needed someone to lean on.

She found her parents' number on the contact list and hit Send.

Just as her father answered, Sarah heard a voice over Sergeant Logan's radio. "We have the body of the victim. It's a dog...."

NINE

Nick thought Sarah was going to collapse when his brother said the word *body*. Instead, she took a deep breath and walked outside.

"Dad, it's Sarah. Have you or Mom talked to Beth recently?"

Nick couldn't hear her father's response, but it clearly wasn't what Sarah wanted to hear. Her shoulders drooped and she started trying to gloss over the urgency of the situation. Finally, she gave up and told her dad the truth. It was painful to watch. Even worse that Nick could do nothing to help.

"Beth was attacked after class last week, but she was okay."

Nick could only imagine what a father would be thinking and asking, and he wished he were in a position to be there for her.

"I'm not sugar-coating it, Dad. She wasn't…" Sarah couldn't even say the word. When she regained her composure, she continued. "Really. Students came out of the building, which scared the assailant off...."

Her father was apparently fully awake now. Nick could hear his deep voice from ten feet away.

"It wasn't my place to tell you," she said softly, as if she could calm him down. "I'm trying to help her, but she does have a mind of her own. I can't watch her twenty-four hours a day. Yes, I'm still on the job."

He could hear voices, but couldn't make out the words. "No, I can't work on the case. Don't even ask that."

Nick could imagine the tension Sarah was feeling now. When his sister had been the target of a drug dealer's revenge, it wasn't easy for any of them to give Kira her independence back. It took a strong woman like his sister to stand up not only to their father, but to Nick and his two brothers—all police officers—when the going got tough.

Nick had only a fleeting minute to question what kind of woman Sarah Roberts was when she replied to something her father said.

"That was Beth's choice, Dad. She didn't want to talk to anyone..." She paused while he responded. "No, I have not changed my opinion, the situation has changed. If you'll let me explain..."

Nick hated this part of the job. Especially when family had to be told bad news over the phone.

"She hasn't answered my calls, my voice messages, nothing. Tonight, I came to check on her...." Sarah paused again, and the spunky former FBI agent turned street cop showed her feminine side.

She started sobbing, then turned and walked down the street, toward her SUV.

Alone.

Nick fought the urge to follow her and offer his support. But he couldn't afford to take the chance of showing feelings for his trainee.

She got inside and lowered her head to the steering wheel.

God, put Your arms around her. Help her to understand why I can't.

Before anything was misunderstood, complicating his career any further, Nick called the shift supervisor and explained the situation, how he'd ended up coming here with his trainee.

"I'll see if one of the female counselors could meet you there to talk to Roberts," his superior offered.

"I'm not necessarily saying she needs someone to talk to as much as someone to act in an official capacity should the situation take a turn for the worst. We still don't know where her sister is." In the background, Nick could hear dispatch calling in.

"Just a minute," the shift supervisor said, then put Nick on hold. Seconds later, he heard dispatch over

Sergeant Logan's radio request backup for a gang related shooting of an officer on the other side of town. Nick was thankful that Garrett was here working this case, and that their older brother was vacationing in the mountains with his family this week.

"Nick, we've got an urgent situation. I'll need to call you back. I know you'll handle Roberts professionally. We don't want to lose either of you," the supervisor said.

Nick put his phone in his pocket and made the difficult decision to stay with his trainee as long as necessary. If she weren't an attractive single female, this wouldn't be an issue. Therefore, he would treat her like any other officer.

The Crime Scene Investigators showed up, talked to Jeremy and drove off. Nick wasn't surprised. An officer-involved shooting was a lot more important than a vandalized car and a murdered dog. He leaned against his brother's patrol car, knowing Garrett was tied up several blocks away, and waited for Sarah to finish her call, repeating "I'm not on duty" over and over to keep himself out of the way of the investigation.

A few minutes later, Sarah approached, appearing emotionally drained. "Sorry that took so long," she said, finding it difficult to look him in the eye. "Anything new?"

"Not a problem. There's been an officer-involved

shooting across town, so the CSI unit was sent over to that scene."

"Oh, is everyone okay?"

"I don't know yet." He'd been so worried about her, he hadn't even asked. "What did you find out?"

"You didn't hear?" She took a deep breath, shaking her head. She leaned a hip against the police cruiser, and Nick fully realized his trainee's beauty and vulnerability. She had as much of a commanding presence out of uniform as she did when tucked into that Kevlar vest and blue uniform, but inside, she was one hundred percent woman.

It wasn't the kind of thing he should notice. And at the same time, he couldn't deny he liked what he saw. He was relieved to see she wasn't as tough as she led her fellow officers to believe. Now that he realized the problem, he could put his guard up and figure out how to keep his own interest under lock and key.

Sarah continued talking, her voice oddly unsteady. "Nothing really. Mom and Dad spoke to her last weekend. They said she had a busy week, so they didn't expect to hear from her until tomorrow night or so. I called my brother, too. He's on his way from Denver, to stay here and wait with me. I want to run home and check my messages, then come back here to meet him. Do you think you could catch a ride back to the station?" she asked with her typical confidence.

"I'm coming with you," he said matter-of-factly. Nick told himself that he had to, until they found her sister. He expected her to argue, but for some reason she seemed relieved. "Too much is going on tonight. I don't want you to be alone." He felt like that gawky sophomore again, stuttering as he talked to the cute senior girl. "How are you doing, Sarah?" He started to put his arm around her, but caught himself. They stood on the front lawn waiting for the officers to finish searching the house.

Sarah wrapped her arms across her chest and rubbed her bare arms. "I know I shouldn't jump to conclusions, but this just doesn't look like she is involved. I think she's off having a great time some-where and will get back and act like nothing's happened. And more than that, she'll think we're crazy to have been concerned." Sarah's lips twitched, and he was glad she was able to maintain a sense of humor despite all she was going through.

As Nick glanced at Sarah, a twinkle of moonlight caught his eyes. He didn't acknowledge the attrac-tion. "Well, while your sister's car being vandalized doesn't appear to have anything to do with her incident the other night, it's not a good coincidence, either. Does she disappear often?"

"Beth is the youngest. She's something of a cru-sader. That she's settled down enough to finish her master's degree is somewhat puzzling, except I think she also sees going on for her Ph.D. as a way to avoid buckling down to get a real job. I just barely think I've figured her out, and then something like this happens and she throws me way off course. She's driving me insane. If she were a criminal, a profiler would lose his job trying to predict what she'd do." Sarah gave him a subtle look of amusement. "I just wanted her to talk to a professional counselor."

Nick laughed at Sarah's assessment of her younger sister. He hoped it all turned out well so she wouldn't look back at this and regret taking it lightly.

"I need to go get my bag and plug my phone in to charge. If she hasn't called back by now, another few minutes won't hurt to be without it."

As Sarah went back to her car, Nick returned to the porch to join Jeremy Logan.

"Is she going to be okay?" Logan asked.

Nick wasn't totally sure he understood why, but his gut told him she was more than all right, that she was more in charge of the situation than any of the rest of them. "Yeah, she'll be fine."

"Man, this is a little freaky. This, then a gang member shooting at Sergeant Mitchell… It's not a good night," Logan said. "Do you know what her sister's other case was about?"

"She told me a little. It's Sarah's call how much to share. We definitely need to keep an eye on the house for a few days. It seems pretty unlikely that the two incidences are not connected, but then again, it doesn't appear that the house has been touched. Why?" Nick studied the surrounding houses, concerned that this area had never been targeted by gangs before.

"This looks a lot like the gang initiations we've seen this month. It could be a coincidence. Her sister isn't in a gang, is she?"

Nick shook his head. "I doubt it. She's in graduate school. Maybe it's a warning. Did you find anything inside?"

"No signs of an intruder in the house, but the stuffed animal out of the car doesn't quite fit with gang activities, either. We'll report it to the detective, see what they can figure out." Jeremy glanced down the street, to see that Sarah had gotten into her car. "Where's she going?"

Nick felt a sudden panic. She wouldn't take off, would she? But she merely pulled forward and parked in front of her sister's house, restoring his confidence in her. "She wants to stay here and wait for her brother. I'm going to wait with her until he arrives. We'll call you if there's any concern."

Jeremy nodded as Sarah joined them at the front door. "Sounds good. We'll get things outside cleaned up and get back on the road."

After a quick look around the outside of the

house, worry returned to Sarah's face. "It makes no sense, Nick. The house hasn't been touched, but the damage to the car seems too personal *not* to be connected. And why is there no indication of where she is?"

Nick motioned for her to go inside first then closed the door and made sure it was locked. "Does your sister have a boyfriend? Maybe she feels safer with him around…."

Her eyes opened wide and she shook her head. "Oh, no. Not Beth. She wouldn't spend the night at his place. They met at church. I think they're both leaders of the youth group. Beth is, anyway. She takes her vow of abstinence very seriously. That's part of why I'm so concerned about what happened the other night. Even though she was spared the worst, the assault was an attack on something that she held dear." Sarah paced the main floor, studying every detail intently.

"How's she dealing with it?"

Sarah hesitated to answer. "She's denying any reaction. I'm worried about how she'll handle it when she realizes what could have happened. I want to get her to talk to a good assault counselor, before someone tries to convince her that *she* did something to deserve this." Sarah's voice became softer and harder to hear.

She was speaking like someone who knew what

her sister was going through. Nick wasn't sure how to respond. "Did anyone in our department say something like that?"

She looked up in confusion; her attention had been somewhere else. "What?"

He wanted to change the question, but didn't. He wanted to take this tiny woman with more spunk than most officers and hold her, comfort her.

He couldn't.

He shouldn't.

He had to find a way to turn off the personal feelings he was discovering for this petite spitfire.

He repeated the question.

"I don't know. She won't talk to me. She won't let me talk to her…." Sarah's voice trembled. Tears stung her eyes, and she fought to cover the fact.

"It's happened to you, hasn't it?"

She turned away. "I didn't say that."

"Not directly, but you sound as if you know what she's going through. Or did you handle serial crimes at the FBI?"

"No, and no. A roommate in college was raped, while I was across the hall sleeping. I'll never forget hearing her scream, seeing the rapist disappear back through that window. I was so terrified, I did everything wrong, ruined the investigation. I vowed I'd never do that again."

"Forgive me for jumping to the wrong conclusion." He couldn't imagine how helpless Sarah must have felt. It was no wonder she wanted to help her sister now. "I'm sorry, Sarah."

He forced his mind to the situation at hand.

"Beth is a youth counselor, encouraging abstinence. Avoiding temptation. She wouldn't stay at Steve's house, even after this. She didn't want to tell our parents, so I'm positive she wouldn't tell her fiancé, either. That concerns me."

"Do you think that's pertinent to the case?" He felt his investigative instincts kick in.

She nodded. "It's worth considering."

"Does she teach abstinence in her college classes, too? It seems I've seen something about an organization promoting abstinence recently, at church, or in the newspaper or somewhere."

Sarah was silent, then started looking around. "Do you see my sister's laptop? It's usually right here."

Nick searched the room. "Maybe she took it with her."

"Hmm. She doesn't usually do so unless she's gone for a holiday or something. Even then, she takes her files on her flash drive and uses Mom and Dad's computer when she's there."

Sarah ran up the stairs and returned a few minutes later, empty-handed.

What was her sister doing, and why hadn't she told Sarah she was going somewhere?

TEN

After her brother showed up, Sarah tried to escape while Nick was talking to Joel.

"Call me when you get to your place, Sarah," her brother said as she quietly closed the screen door.

Nick swung around and darted out after her. "Wait a minute there! Talk to you later, Joel."

Her brother laughed from the doorway as Sarah hurried to her SUV with Nick running behind. "Keep a close eye on my sister, Nick."

"That's easier said than done." He knocked on the passenger window and pointed to the seat, and Sarah smiled as she unlocked the door.

He climbed inside. "What was that about? I told you I'm going to be your shadow until we figure this out."

"I was just trying to give myself a fighting chance to get away," she said firmly, trying not to laugh. "I meant what I said about not jeopardizing your career, Nick. I want you to leave this problem to me. Don't get involved. How else can I prove to you that I'm not trying to get you into trouble?"

"Why do you care what I think?" he challenged.

"Because you're my training officer," she replied automatically. She started the engine, realizing she didn't know for sure why she cared. Yes, she'd had a crush on him in high school, but she'd also had a crush on about a dozen other boys back then, and the thought of them didn't turn butterflies loose in her stomach.

"Maybe you need to take a few days off until this is under control."

"Maybe I should," she said, rather than arguing that she'd have had no issue with pursuing this, even if it meant pushing the limits with her previous field training officer. It was Nick she didn't want hurt in the cross fire. She wanted to protect him as much as she did her family. She had three more weeks as his trainee. Another four after that with another officer, on her last probationary rotation. It seemed like forever, and she couldn't wait to have her independence back.

Nick was painfully quiet, and she was glad for the darkness. Unfortunately, they were accustomed to the dark, and even in the cover of the night, she felt vulnerable to this man.

She pulled up at her apartment and got out. The

long day was taking its toll, and the adrenaline churned up by her sister's disappearance was wearing off. Still, Sarah knew she needed to find some information about Beth's whereabouts before she'd be able to sleep.

"Why doesn't your sister normally take her laptop with her?" Nick said as he followed Sarah up the steps.

It seemed like an odd question to come out of the blue. "I don't know. Why do you ask?"

He held the screen while she unlocked her door. "I'm just curious why you think it's so odd that it's gone. Laptops are made to carry along."

She shrugged. "It just is. Over Christmas, she went the full month at our parents' without it. It's an older machine, so maybe it's not very fast. I don't know."

"Is she a heavy e-mailer?"

Sarah spun around, annoyed. "I don't need you tempting me to dig into her investigation, Nick."

He smiled. "I'm not trying to tempt you. I'm trying to point out that it's possible she went someplace where she didn't think she would have computer access. Or maybe she e-mailed you. When is the last time you checked?" He glanced over at her desk and raised an eyebrow. "I know you haven't since you got to work. We had the interview of the bank robbers before briefing...."

"And didn't have a break all night. I hope you're right." Sarah hurried to her computer and pressed the power button. "While it's revving up, how about I put a pizza in the oven? We never did eat tonight."

He glanced around the unsettled apartment, curious to learn more about his partner, she supposed. "The last thing you want is dishes. I'll call for one. What do you like on it?"

She paused, realizing how Nick still fit the image she'd had of him in high school. He'd been one of the quiet guys who hadn't let his talent go to his head. He'd grown into a sweet, considerate gentleman. A man of honor.

He was still waiting for her answer. "On your pizza, what do you like?"

"Oh, sorry. I was thinking about something. Anything but pineapple and anchovies. I'm going to change and pack a few things for overnight."

Before he could respond, she'd disappeared up the stairs. He had the local pizza place programmed in his cell phone, so he called the order in, and waited for her to return. Boxes from her move were still stacked around the living room and kitchen. She had a few photos out on the mantel of the gas fireplace. He recognized her brother, and guessed the woman to be her sister, though she didn't look much like Sarah. Beth was a few inches taller, with a short, sporty hairstyle and lighter hair. Another photo was pushed to the back of the shelf, lying facedown. Nick picked it up and peeked at the photo of Sarah and a man on the beach.

"That's trash," Sarah said from behind him.

He turned, almost dropping the picture. Sarah had brushed her hair so that it hung, lush and gleaming, around her shoulders. "What is?"

"The whole thing. The relationship, the cutesy frame…" She took the photo from him and tossed it into the trash can. "I had the movers pack for me. That wouldn't have made it here if I'd done it myself."

"You don't owe me an explanation," he said, though he was happy she'd given it.

She smiled. "I kind of hoped you'd want to know that. I mean, you did tell me not to keep any pertinent information from you."

While he groped for some clever comeback, she went to her computer and entered her password. He wasn't prepared for the sight of her in those clothes—snug jeans and T-shirt, and a pink, fitted jacket. He tried to keep his attention focused on the investigation.

"While the computer logs me onto the network, could I get you something to drink?"

He was encouraged to learn that his earlier assessment of Sarah appeared to be one hundred percent accurate. This woman was in charge. "I ordered a soda with the pizza. I figure it's going to be a long night."

"Morning. It's almost five." She bent forward as the monitor started displaying incoming e-mails.

Nick stepped to the side, careful to keep his distance. He couldn't lose sight of the fact that he was her training officer. Until he could get her reassigned without causing himself more trouble, Sarah Roberts was off-limits. Whether he liked it or not.

"No e-mails from her. I want to check one more thing." Sarah went to a search engine and typed in her sister's name. "There she is, as a contributing author on a 'waiting for marriage' Web site. And on a blog on another site…"

"What's that?"

Sarah looked at the conference link that Nick pointed to. "It's the weekend after next."

"I had hoped that's where she was today."

"No, but maybe she's meeting with the organizers. That's the only thing that makes sense. Let me check her Coedspace listing again, see if she mentions abstinence there." Sarah scrolled through the information, looking for her sister's name. Just then, her doorbell rang.

Nick paid for the delivery and thanked the kid by name. "Ah, nothing like hot pizza at 5:00 a.m. Shall we take it back to eat with Joel?"

"Sure," Sarah said as she shut down her computer. She grabbed her bag and met Nick at the entryway. He stepped out the screen door, holding it while she locked the dead bolt.

"Did you check your phone messages?" he asked as an afterthought.

She nodded. "No word yet. I'm certain she's okay, though. I'm sure of it."

"How can you be so positive?"

"I've always known when one of my family was hurt or in trouble. It took years to recognize that sick-to-the-stomach feeling I get, but it's pretty accurate."

"Is it that twin-connection phenomenon?"

She shrugged. "Partially, I suppose, except there's eleven years between Beth and me, so it's not just that."

"Does your brother have it, too?"

She beeped the device to unlock her SUV, and they were off. "Not that he's acknowledged. I don't talk about it much."

"Oh, so you don't want me to mention it to him?"

She laughed. "Not really. They already think I'm the oddball of the family."

"Why's that?" Nick asked, inhaling the tempting aroma of pizza. "Think Joel would notice if we ate it on the way?"

"Yes, and to answer your first question, I'm short. I'm the only one in the family who isn't in education. I—"

"You're the brainiac, and they think you should use it for something less dangerous than law enforcement?"

She looked at him and smiled. "Yeah. They don't understand me, why I find the thrill of the chase so rewarding. The last thing I need is for them to ship me off to the psych hospital to find out why I have a gut instinct."

He'd never made that connection. "So did you know you had this instinct when you were a kid?"

"Not really. I knew when my brother was going to be in big trouble, but that wasn't quite the same. I had usually snitched on him, very covertly, of course, so I had insider information. And I don't want Joel to know that, either."

Nick smiled, his eyes meeting hers. "Remind me not to make you mad."

"As long as we're on the same team, you're safe," she said, turning the final corner to her sister's house.

"Let's keep it that way."

When they pulled into the parking space at the curb, the police cars were gone. The soft glow from the lights inside made the house stand out, even on the fringes of the college campus.

Sarah knocked on the door and waited for her brother to let them in. "Hi, we brought breakfast. Feel like some pizza?"

Joel yawned. "Not really. I'd like some sleep. I don't know how you two can keep these kind of hours. I'm just glad it's Sunday and I don't have to be at school this morning."

Sarah looked over her shoulder and smiled at Nick. Why was it that being with her felt so natural? He hadn't felt this free to be himself in months. Not since his reputation had been called into question.

"We do sleep, it's just during the hours that you're normally herding middle schoolers. Now if there's anyone with a job no one understands, that has to be it," Sarah teased.

"Yeah, and everyone thinks *you're* the tough one," he sparred back.

"I wouldn't want to go up against her in a brawl," Nick interjected. "Have you seen your sister in action?"

Joel glanced at him. "I had to share a womb with her. She's been kicking and punching all her life! But no, I haven't seen her in a fight recently, thankfully. She's still a little spitfire, huh?"

"That's an accurate description," Nick said with a laugh. "So do you teach, or coach, or…?"

Her brother yawned again. "Both. I teach science and coach basketball and track."

They visited for a few minutes, then, after the pizza had been devoured, Sarah asked Joel if the police had stopped in to discuss anything.

"Nick's brother wants him to call. A tow truck took her car to the police investigations something or other. That's about all they told me. So what do you think really went down?"

Nick looked at Sarah, curious as to what she'd say.

"We're not really investigating either of the cases, Joel, and even if we were, you know I can't talk about evidence. I'm only here because I'm her sister."

Joel accepted that, but still pressed for more information. Sarah said nothing more than Nick had heard her say before, and no more than he would have told his family if he were in the same situation. He had learned a lot from his sister Kira's experience, and respected the way her fiancé, Dallas, had handled her case. All had ended well for them personally, too.

"Nick?"

"What?" Why was he so easily distracted tonight?

"My mom and dad will be here this afternoon. Would you mind if Joel and I get some sleep? You can take my SUV back to the station if you—"

"I'm not going anywhere. You two go on upstairs. I'll watch out here for a while, then grab a few minutes' rest. Since we're off Monday night, we can catch up on last night's paperwork, and hopefully, have some answers on your sister by the end of the day."

Joel studied them both. "You don't expect anyone to come back after all that, do you?"

Nick explained. "Vandals often do come back, either to finish a job, to show off that they carried out on the act, or…"

Joel looked at Sarah. "You didn't say this was gang related."

"No, I didn't. We don't know that it is. It's too soon to know any of that for sure," she said.

Nick knew it was unlikely that they'd learn any more over the course of his brother's shift, but he made the offer, anyway. "I'm going to call Garrett, see what they found out. I should hear back from him before you wake up."

Nick watched the twins walk up the stairs together, hoping he'd have better news about their sister before the rest of their family arrived. He turned out the lights and sat on the futon, hoping to catch someone coming back to the scene of the crime. Every few minutes he went to the rear of the house and peered out the kitchen window. He called Garrett and left a message, eager for any news at this point. Anything that would help him stay awake.

Nick drank another glass of soda, figuring that between the sugar and the caffeine, he'd be able to make it through till daylight, when the likelihood of the suspects returning would lessen. Surveillance never had been his specialty.

The first few trips from the living room to the kitchen were dicey, as he tried to make his way without tripping over Beth's piles of books or breaking anything. Including his own leg, which he cracked on her old trunk more than once when cutting the corner too close.

Just as the sun rose, he felt the sugar wearing off. His eyes drifted closed, and this time, he couldn't fight it. He slept soundly, the occasional snore startling him into a more comfortable position.

He woke to screams at the front door, his phone ringing, and the subject of his dreams rushing into the room with her weapon drawn.

Nick jumped from the futon and tripped over the trunk serving as a coffee table.

He peeled his eyes open, realizing Sarah was pointing a gun at him, then at her sister.

"It's me! Nick!" he cried.

"Nick?" Sarah asked.

At the same moment her sister said, "Sarah? What are you doing here, who is Nick, and why are the two of you in my house?"

ELEVEN

Sarah tucked her gun in her waistband and rushed toward her sister. "Where have you been? Why haven't you returned my phone calls? We were worried sick."

"We? As in you and *Nick?*" She looked at him as if he were the enemy. "Who is he?"

Nick stepped forward, offering his hand. "I'm Sarah's training officer."

Just then Joel made his way down the stairs. "Is it safe to come down? All of the weapons put away?"

Sarah brushed the hair off her forehead. "You're such a dork."

"Joel? What are you doing here?" Beth asked.

"You may as well set your things down, kiddo," he answered. "This is going to take awhile. And about the time Sarah finishes the story, Mom and Dad should be here and we can go through it all again." He gave his little sister a hug and took her bags. "At least you're okay."

"You told them?" Beth yelled. "Sarah!"

Nick's phone rang, and he stepped outside to answer it, away from the fury of Sarah's sister.

Sarah knew there was no better time than the present to explain what had unfolded in Beth's absence. It wasn't going to get any easier. When she was through, she looked at her sister, who was white as a ghost.

"I can't believe you told anyone what happened, let alone Mom and Dad and Joel," Beth said, covering her face with her hands. "I trusted you to keep this between us."

"Hold on, Beth. You can't expect Sarah to take that burden on herself," Joel interrupted. "It's been a week, and you wouldn't answer your phone. You didn't call her back. What was she supposed to think? I'm not even a cop, and I'd fear the worst under these circumstances." He gave their sister a firm lecture about them being family and how much it hurt that she'd piled all this pressure onto Sarah.

Beth crossed her arms over her chest and began to pout like a two-year-old. "I just want to forget about it and put it behind me. Is that too much to ask for?"

"Yes, Beth," Sarah was saying as Nick walked back inside. "It's unrealistic and irresponsible…."

His face was drawn, with a seriousness she'd not seen before. She looked at him, waiting for him to

say something. When he didn't, she continued dril-
ling her sister, despite being distracted by the feeling
that something worse had happened. "So, how were
we supposed to react to your sudden disappearance
and the vandalism to your property?" she asked.
"Not to mention finding your name and address
listed on Coedspace?"

"I figured it's on every other online directory.
What's the point of making more work for kids who
want to contact me? But fine, I'll take it off if it will
make you happy."

Nick interrupted. "No, call the detective now,
before you remove her address from the Web site.
Otherwise, they won't be able to use it in the investigation, if it turns out to be related."

"My sister's safety comes first," Sarah argued.

"Of course it does, but do you know she'll be safe
even if you remove her listing? If the suspect did get
her address off the Web site, the damage is already
done. That was Garrett on the phone, by the way." He
turned to Beth. "I can't say why, but I think you need
to move in with your sister or someone until the assailant is caught. You're putting yourself and Sarah
both in jeopardy. Last night it was your car. Next
time, it may not be quite as easy to repair the damage."

Sarah looked at Nick, wondering what had happened to make him lecture her sister. It was nice to
have him support her, but he'd gone a little far.

Beth stared at the stranger giving her orders. She glanced at Sarah, then eased toward the stairs in silence.

"Go pack your bags, Beth. You can stay at my place for now," Sarah told her.

Joel led their sister upstairs while Sarah talked to Nick. "What happened?"

"There was a rape. The woman from two houses down went out to get her dog to quit barking. She heard someone bashing up the car and went to get the dog, which had broken through the fence. The suspect attacked her, told her to give the 'prude' who lives here a message from him."

Sarah clapped her hand to her mouth. "He knows…"

Nick took her into his arms and held her close. "We have to catch this guy. He chased the victim down the alley. She said her dog tried to protect her. He bit the suspect and held on to his leg, and she was able to break away. He was apparently dragging the dog, and when she escaped, he shot it. By then, she'd gone into a convenience store and called the police."

"It could have been Beth. How do I tell her that her neighbor was…"

Nick let Sarah go. "If that's not enough to get through to her, nothing will. But then again, I don't want her to blame herself, either."

Sarah nodded, wiping the tears from her eyes as she put some distance between them. "Any similarities to the other attacks?"

"You'll have to talk to the detectives about that. I don't know enough about the other incidents, but I wouldn't feel comfortable with my sister living here, especially by herself. And I don't feel comfortable with you living here with her, either."

Nick looked at her with his soft gray eyes, and for a minute she felt something more than the brotherhood of the badge between them. Then he glanced away, and she realized it was dangerous to even imagine a romance with her training officer. She had to get Nick Matthews out of her head. She had to get her mind back on the subject.

"She won't even let me suggest that this might be someone she knew, let alone convince her that she needs to make changes to her life. I'm surprised that she listened to you."

"You and Beth will both have to talk to the detectives, Sarah. They have to consider all of this if we're going to catch him."

There was a long pause. "She works mainly with the girls in the abstinence group," Sarah murmured at last. "Maybe it's one of their boyfriends."

"That's warped, but I've heard of worse. You can't fly under the radar on this. It's dangerous for you, for Beth and for your career." He crossed his arms over his chest, his blue T-shirt clinging to his body. Sarah reminded herself that he shouldn't even be here.

She heard Joel and Beth moving around upstairs, then turned and walked to the kitchen. She glanced outside for the first time since the crime scene had been cleared. "Not to mention *your* career, right?"

"Don't make this about me," Nick said, leaning against the doorjamb. "I know how difficult it is to leave this to someone else when you have the experience to handle the case. It's a fine line to walk. A dangerous line. You can think you're in control, and in one moment of distraction, it's all gone."

Sarah glanced up the stairs. "Is that what happened to you?"

"I didn't professionally interfere with the investigation, but I was definitely keeping my nose in the details and keeping an eye out for my sister's safety. I was working a drug investigation at the same time. I left myself wide-open when I asked the two officers to tag some evidence instead of doing it myself."

"Live and learn," Sarah said softly.

"I'd rather you not learn that same lesson the hard way. Would your sister listen to someone else? Like my sister, maybe? After her incident, Kira is volunteering with the county victim's advocacy network. I hear she's doing a great job helping out there."

Sarah took a few steps toward the stairs and shook her head. "I don't know what would reach Beth right now, but I know she's going to blame herself for her neighbor's assault. You got through to her without even telling her that. Maybe Kira could, too. I just know that I have to find something that will make her understand how serious this is."

TWELVE

The next day, Nick met Sarah at the police station to finish their reports. "How's your sister doing?"

"Considering my parents won't stop asking her questions, she's hanging in there. I haven't told her about the neighbor yet. But I think she's finally willing to talk to someone."

"And you? How're you holding up?"

"The same. It's a small apartment for four people." She printed off the last report and started reading it for accuracy, then handed it to Nick. "They're out looking for a more secure, bigger place for us to share." Sarah took a deep breath and let it out slowly, as if she was counting to ten.

Nick glanced at the report, then peered up at her. "And how is that settling with you and Beth?"

She shrugged. "It's fine, I guess. I just wish it were something we had a little more control over. Dad isn't going to leave till he's moved us both.

Either that, or until we consent to go to Montana with him and Mom and never leave home again!"

"Montana was the hideout of the Unabomber. You can always use that as an argument not to do so."

Sarah laughed. "Thank you. I'm not going, but bigger and more secure is hard to find these days."

"It sounds like a good idea, though. My sister has a place in a gated community. I think there's a three-bedroom condo for sale. They're pretty nice, in a good neighborhood. Even a gate doesn't keep everyone out, though."

"Don't tell my dad that, please. I just want to find someplace soon. I haven't signed a lease for my apartment yet, so I need to make a decision pronto. I stayed with Beth till I found something, and just barely got moved in myself, but it's definitely not going to work for the two of us. Beth's been in her house for two years, so she's fine to give her notice. Under the circumstances, I figure it's safer to make it look like she's living there for a while longer anyway, until this guy is caught."

"Stop right there. That sounds like you're planning something, Sarah." He almost wished they were assigned to patrol tonight, given the stress she had waiting at home. "Did you call the detective yet?" He glanced up from the report to find her looking at him.

"It's not quite that easy, Nick." She ran her hand through her hair and pressed her lips together.

"Why not? These details could break the case," he said, handing the paper back to her. "This report looks good, by the way."

"The whole thing could also come back to bite me. I want to fit in here. I want the other officers to give me a chance. I can't come in and act like a hotshot from the FBI, telling the detectives how to do their jobs." She shook her head. "I've left a message for Detective Wang to call me. I mentioned that Beth is staying with me now, but he hasn't phoned back yet. He didn't recognize me when I picked my sister up after the incident, and for all I know, he may not even realize I'm a cop for FCPD."

Nick looked at her, shook his head and smiled. "That's kind of funny, a detective who didn't recognize a coworker. Even I recognized you from fourteen years ago." He didn't dare admit to her that he'd been too shy fourteen years ago to ask an older woman out.

"With a little reminder," she said with a grin. "I thought I'd see how he responds when I talk to him. If he seems irritated, I'll find some other way to pass the information along. I'm just not willing to make waves right now."

Nick wrote down his sister's phone number and the cross streets where her condo was located, and handed it to Sarah. "There were several weeks between each attack until Beth's and her neighbor's. If the online community is how the perp is finding his victims, we need to take action right now. I don't care if Wang doesn't like someone thinking of something he hasn't. Our goal is to solve the case and prevent more assaults." Nick gazed at her again. "I understand your hesitation, but this is not something you can keep quiet about, Sarah. Take it to the shift supervisor if you don't want to step on Wang's toes. Send Lieutenant Douglas an e-mail with your discoveries. Let him look into it and pass it along."

"I notice *you're* not willing to tell Wang." Her eyes sparkled. "You think he's going to be upset?"

"He and I worked okay together, but I think it will come better from someone else right now. Like you. I know it's hard to swim upstream with your hands tied behind your back. But one way or another, it's a lead that needs to be passed along." Nick studied Sarah's face. "You shouldn't back down. Your experience is worth a lot in a department like Fossil Creek. You can't hide your skills in a place like this or you'll be kicked around forever. And it seems like you are trying to hide them. What's going on?"

She didn't answer, just shrugged.

Nick wasn't up for games right now. He'd overstepped the lines already. If she wasn't going to come clean with what she was up to, he wasn't about to drop his guard.

"When we return to work on Thursday, I want some answers. And I'd better not see you holding back. Talk about something coming back to bite you, that's going to be it." He stood, pushing the chair aside. "Have a good weekend."

"You too, Nick," he heard her say as the door closed behind him. "Sorry I can't be who you want me to be."

Nick opened the local newspaper Friday morning, and nearly choked on his coffee. "Rapist Taunts Fossil Creek Police, Promises to Strike Again." He had spent his days off splitting firewood for his wood stove, ignoring the outside world, trying to put Sarah Roberts out of his mind. So much for his efforts. She was front and center once more.

Had she talked to anyone about her suspicions yet? What had spurred this change in the suspect's pattern?

He called Garrett to see what he knew about the message the newspaper was referring to. "Did it mention anyone specifically?" he asked his brother.

"All we were told last night was that until he's caught, we're patrolling in pairs. The chief's job is on the line, I suppose. They've asked for volunteers to work the Harvest Festival tonight. I think they wanted to cancel it altogether."

Nick left early for work, hoping to talk to Sarah before the briefing. He'd called yesterday to find out about her house hunt, and had left her a message, reminding her to be prepared for a lot of walking the downtown carnival grounds during the festival the next two nights. It seemed like a perfect place for their rapist to strike, especially after his recent message to the newspaper. Nick also needed to be sure she'd talked to Detective Wang.

He turned onto Highway 87 and noticed a car on the shoulder with the trunk lid open and the left side lifted on a jack. He looked at his watch and started to drive past, until he saw the white-haired woman trying to turn the wrench to loosen the lug nuts on the wheel.

Pulling off the road, he called the station to let them know he'd be a little late, and give his location in case they'd already received a report of a stranded motorist. He tugged his wallet from his pocket to show the woman his badge. "Good evening. I'm Sergeant Matthews from Fossil Creek Police Department. Looks like you could use some help."

"I'd just about given up and started walking," the woman said. "No one stops to help these days."

"You never know whether it's safer if they do or don't. Do you have roadside assistance to change that for you?"

She looked at him as if he was speaking a foreign

language. "I don't even have one of those cellular phones, or I'd have called for help. No one even stopped to offer to call someone for me."

He could see where this conversation was going—in circles. "Let's see if we can get you back on the road then." He lowered the jack.

"I just got the car lifted. Why're you doing that?"

"To keep the tire from turning while I loosen the lug nuts. Where's your spare?"

She shrugged. "I don't have one. My husband put this jack in the trunk before he died, I guess, but I can't find the extra tire."

Nick paused. She was obviously confused. It was going to be a long night. He asked a few general questions to make sure she wasn't disoriented, then went back to the topic of the tire when he felt sure she was okay. "You certain there's no spare? Mind if I take a look? They're usually under the floor of the trunk these days."

"Be my guest, but I didn't see anything in there. My husband used to keep track of these things."

Nick simply smiled, remembering the days when his grandmother didn't touch her car. A minute later he was lifting the mat in her trunk and detaching the spare tire.

"Well, I'll be. I wonder if Gordon knew that was there."

Nick smiled again, reminded of the days when

a spare tire had been full size and few people hesitated to stop and help a neighbor. Times had definitely changed.

From there, things went smoothly, and he had the tire changed in a matter of minutes. "Be sure to take this in and get it repaired right away—today or tomorrow. These spares aren't made for driving long distances on." He looked at his watch and reminded the woman that the tire shop two miles up the road was only open until six.

"Thank you very much, Officer. We need more people like you around," she said before she drove off.

Heading toward work again, Nick grew more and more concerned as he thought about how easy it was for someone stranded to be victimized. How frightened people were of lending a helping hand. It seemed these days most people assumed everyone on the road owned a cell phone. That they were obligated to, for their own safety and convenience.

His department needed to do more to educate the public on safety and public services available, he decided as he drove into the lot, noticing most of the cruisers had already left on patrol.

The shift supervisor met him as he walked into the station. "I sent Roberts out to the festival with Thomas and Daniels, so as soon as you're dressed, get downtown and meet up with her." He started to walk away, then stopped. "Oh, you'll notice on the assignment board, we're doubling up on patrols until this rapist is stopped. So until further notice, you and Roberts are a team. If it lasts past her rotation with you, so be it. The mayor has instructed the chief that we're to make immediate and substantial changes."

Nick noted the sarcasm in the supervisor's voice. "Or heads will roll, huh?"

"Something like that. And good job, by the way, sending Roberts to talk to me about her observations. I think she's onto something with that online angle. All three victims had postings on that Coedspace. Wang is looking into it."

Nick was relieved that Sarah had followed through, but he was still concerned. "Good," he said, hesitant to mention that Wang despised using computers, so it wasn't likely he'd be very effective investigating a digital connection between the cases. "If I can do anything to help…"

"Thanks for the offer," his supervisor said with a smile. "The chief is looking for someone who can handle the computer side of the case, to work with Wang."

Nick nodded. "I'm glad to hear it. And by the way, I'd like to talk with you sometime about holding a few community safety classes. It's been a long time since we've given any."

"I'll pass that suggestion along and have them get in touch with you. It's a good idea."

"I think Officer Roberts would be willing to help, too."

"Good. I'll add you both to the list. Stay safe out there."

Downtown businesses were bustling with festival goers when Nick arrived ten minutes later. He radioed Sarah to find out her location, and found her with Sergeant Donovan, her previous training officer. The three walked together for a few blocks, making few contacts during the first part of their shift.

As the night went on, however, gang members were an ominous presence, and half the manpower was used to keep crosstown rivals apart. There were three thefts in stores, two wallets pickpocketed, a half-dozen fights and one medical emergency. By the time the carnival wound down, the officers had been run ragged.

No one had noticed anyone matching the rapist's description. Nick wasn't sure if that was good news or bad.

Sarah had been quiet, considering how busy it had been. They made one last foot patrol after escorting business owners along the carnival perimeter to their cars. As they were headed to their cruiser at two in the morning, a minivan pulled into the alley behind the downtown bakery.

"Everyone else is leaving, and a van is pulling in. That's odd," Nick said. "I think we'd better check on it."

Sarah radioed in their location and both of them hurried toward the vehicle. A young woman jumped out of the van and headed toward the building, then screamed.

THIRTEEN

"Police!" Nick yelled.

He drew his Glock and searched for what she was screaming at.

The blonde dropped her backpack and threw her arms into the air, then screamed again at the top of her lungs. "Don't shoot!"

Sarah pulled out her flashlight and quickly scanned the creepy alley with the halogen light, finally settling the beam on the girl with her hands in the air. "Are you okay?"

"What?"

"It's all right, miss. Put your arms down. We're police officers." Sarah lowered her heavy-duty flashlight, training the light on the ground.

The blonde put her hand out to shade her eyes. "Oh, I couldn't see you, I just saw a gun pointed at me and two figures. It freaked me out."

Nick pulled out his own flashlight and walked

past the two of them. "I'm going to take a look down here."

"Sorry about the scare," Sarah said to the woman. "We saw your van driving into the alley and wanted to make sure everything was okay. Are you going in here alone?"

Her eyes were still as big as saucers as she stepped under the mercury light above the bakery door, her hands still elevated. "Yes. I make the pastries for the bakery," she said breathlessly.

"Go ahead and put your hands down," Sarah said as she rested her palm on her gun, just in case Nick needed backup.

He had disappeared down the alley, making sure no one was lurking in the shadows. "Clear," he said as he headed back. He radioed dispatch, updating them on their location.

"We're warning everyone in the college vicinity to be on the lookout for a man fitting this description," Sarah said quietly as she held up a sketch of the suspect from the rape earlier in the week. "Do you come in at this time every day?"

The blond woman nodded.

"Alone?" This girl was either very brave or very ignorant.

"The owner is upstairs in the apartment, but Grandma doesn't hear much."

"Again, I'm sorry we scared you. Why don't we

check out the shop for you, make sure no one slipped in during the festival," Nick offered. "We'd be happy to request increased patrols through here, about this time, but I'd recommend you call the police department and ask for someone to meet you every morning to make sure you get in safely."

"Especially until we catch the rapist," Sarah added.

"Thanks. It's usually pretty quiet when I come in. If I see anyone lingering, I drive around a few minutes until they leave." She picked up her backpack and keys, fumbling to find the right one, then unlocked the door and invited them inside. "Mrs. Scott, my grandmother, gets the dough started before she goes to bed, then when I arrive I roll it out and bake the pastries."

Nick shone his light up the stairway to the owner's apartment.

"Then I decorate the cakes for the next day. Grandmother has been training me to take over for her when I buy the shop."

"That's a huge undertaking for someone so young," Sarah commented.

The blonde set down her backpack and jacket. "Yes, I suppose it is. I'm a party planner, so the shop will be making a few transformations. I think Fossil Creek is ready for the change. Either of you know anyone who's getting married, send them to me."

She watched as Nick searched the kitchen and then walked past her into the customer area, checking to be sure the front doors were locked.

"Would you mind helping me carry a box, Officer…" she looked at Nick's badge as he returned "…Matthews? I'm going to change it into a party planning shop. It was a last-minute idea to have some costumes here for the festival tonight. I'm hoping to spark some interest in them before Halloween. With all our health-conscious customers, the bakery isn't going to survive on its own."

"Sure," he said, following her to the van and back inside with a cumbersome box. "I'd suggest you consider having them shipped directly here in the future so you don't have to unload in the middle of the night. I can't believe your grandmother slept through your screaming. Should we check on her?"

The blonde looked at Sarah, then Nick. "She's a heavy sleeper. She never even wakes up when I'm down here running the mixers and clanking pans. You'd probably give her a heart attack by going up there." She reached for a stiff white apron, unfolded it and slipped it over her head. "I saw the headlines this morning. Is the rapist in this area?"

"We're just being cautious," Sarah said, "but coming and going in the middle of the night isn't a great idea right now. And be sure not to open the door for anyone when you're here alone."

"Thanks for the warning," she said. "If you'd like to come back in a couple of hours, I'll have some pastries and doughnuts ready. My treat."

"Thanks, but we're going off duty soon. I'll ask the next shift to keep an eye out for you here, though." Sarah eyed the box of costumes. "Could I get your name so we can let them know who we contacted?"

"Amber Scott," she said hesitantly, as she tied the apron around her waist. "I'm not going to be in any report or anything, am I?"

"Not unless something else happens," Sarah answered.

"Oh, good. I don't want to raise any issues, with this sale going through." She put a hairnet over the bun on the top of her head and walked them to the door. "Thanks again."

They could hear the heavy metal door lock click behind them. As they walked back to their patrol car at the other end of the alley, Sarah had an idea of how to get a better sense of what was really going on at the festival the next night.

Nick pulled out his notepad and jotted down Amber Scott's name. "That was interesting."

"And I thought my sister was bubbly. That much energy makes my head hurt."

"She's young yet. Give her some time, especially

with everything she hopes to do in her shop." Nick rolled his eyes. "It's hard to imagine Mrs. Scott's bakery as a perky party place."

Sarah laughed.

"You ought to laugh more often, Roberts. It looks good on you," he said.

"What, you think the brainiac can't have a sense of humor?"

"I didn't mean that. It's been a rough few weeks, and it's good to see you smile for a change."

"You should be funny more often then. I happen to like laughing."

That quieted him down, and it was awhile before Sarah asked, "You think the shift supervisor would be willing to let some of the officers go plainclothes tomorrow night? It seemed like we were always one step behind the action tonight. I think that if some of us weren't in uniform, it would be easier to blend in and catch any troublemakers. That goes for un-marked cars, too."

Nick shrugged his broad shoulders. "I don't know. It's worth asking. He'd need to let everyone know who's on duty, since we wouldn't be as easily identified."

"That's exactly the point."

"So how's your sister doing?"

"Reality finally hit her when she found out about her neighbor. Beth can't stand the thought of going back to her house now, even to move. Dad and I went over yesterday and picked up a few things. We're closing on the condo soon, by the way. Thanks for telling us about it. It's going to be a good move for us both, I think."

"Good. Kira will love having new neighbors. Her fiancé is also a cop, with the Antelope Springs PD. I'll introduce you sometime."

Sarah unlocked the cruiser and both of them got inside, anxious to call it a night. After she'd e-mailed her idea to the shift supervisor, she went home feeling pretty positive.

When she arrived, Beth was still awake, playing computer games. "Hi, how was your night?" Sarah asked as she plopped onto the sofa.

Her sister shrugged.

"How did the class work online tonight?"

"I didn't do it. I sent them my e-mail address to send assignments to."

Sarah felt the relief of finding a new condo and the few minutes of laughter she'd shared with Nick drain from her like cold, murky water. "What happened? It seemed like a good alternative for the moment."

"I was fine until you started mothering me. Are you happy now? It's bothering me. I'm afraid to talk to anyone, online or in person, wondering if that's how this guy found me. You have me terrified."

Sarah suspected that was an excuse, but she didn't argue. Beth needed someone to be angry with, and right now, that was her. "And what do you want to do about it?"

Beth shrugged, trying to hold back tears. Not the first today, apparently, from the look of her eyes. "Just give me some space."

Sarah nodded, counting to ten. "We've given you space, and you can see how that worked for us. I've barely seen you since meeting you at the hospital the night it happened. It *should* be bothering you—it's a serious crime. It's also time to get in to see a counselor. I doubt that you ever heard about the time my roommate in Boulder was raped right across the hall while I slept."

Beth looked at her with wide eyes and shook her head.

"Some guy broke into our apartment through her window and put his hand over her mouth. He had a knife and threatened to use it if she didn't cooperate."

"Why didn't you tell me about that?"

"This is the first time you've let me talk to you, Beth. I've wanted to tell you that I know what you're going through. I haven't been assaulted like you were, but I've worked with a lot of victims who have been. I never told you before because you were so young when it happened, Mom and Dad didn't want you to know, and then I guess it didn't really come up." Sarah knew this might be her best chance to talk to her sister. Though she was tired and had another long night ahead of her, she needed this more than sleep.

"I'm sorry I've acted like a brat, Sarah. I just wanted to forget it ever happened. I didn't want to think about how close I came to this changing my life."

"I understand that, Beth, but it has changed your life. It should. You can choose to use this to reach out to others, help raise awareness…."

"No, I couldn't. I don't want to let anyone think I'm a poor example. I mean, I must have—"

Sarah knew what she was going to say. "No, Beth, you didn't do anything to deserve this. Most sexual assaults aren't about the sex. It's violence. It's a warped person acting out violence toward someone who for some reason triggers this anger inside them." She hugged her sister. "I'm sorry I didn't get that through to you earlier. I'm not blaming you at all. It's really difficult to discuss assault with someone so close, because so much between us can be applied to situations that, on the outside, look like they're the same, but they're not."

Beth gazed at her through tear-filled eyes. "What?"

"That's a perfect example of what I was trying to

say. If I give a watered-down example of what I know, clinically and criminally, about sexual predators, you'll either take it personally, because you think I'm talking directly to you about some incident that I'm remembering, or you'll get angry and shut me out. I'm not trying to throw out accusations. I don't want to counsel you. I want you to go to a professional counselor, Beth."

"Fine. I'll find one tomorrow."

"I want you to think about something else, too. I'm not pointing fingers. I just want you to look at this through a different perspective. I know that you believe abstinence is the only way to remain pure, but there are a lot of women who don't have that option. Someone stole their innocence from them, like this creep threatened to do to you. There are a lot of people who need the healing that a Waiting for Marriage support group might be able to offer. With your conference next weekend, it's a perfect chance to bring this into a discussion. If you're interested, I know a speaker who would do a good job."

"We already have—"

"I know," Sarah said. "You have all your speakers lined up. But I keep asking God why this happened to you. I've never known anyone to be upset with you over anything," she said gently. "Yet this guy has come after you twice, Beth, and the second time he sent a pretty strong message of why you're his target."

"I don't want to know."

"I won't get graphic, but your work for purity is the only thing that makes sense to me. Think of how powerful messages are sent, Beth. Through a strong person who has faced his or her fears and shares that enlightenment with others. You can use this for God. You're one of God's missionaries. When you're doing God's work, the devil sends out the troops. This creep who assaulted you is trying to stop the good work you're doing. And if you hold back from doing it, if you hide your head, he's going to win."

Beth wiped her eyes and wrapped her arms around Sarah. "I didn't know you were a believer— I mean, still…."

"I know what you mean. I got pretty lazy about it for a while. Since your assault, God and I have been discussing a lot of things. It's helped having a partner who isn't afraid to pray when things get ugly."

"He seems like a good guy, judging from the one time I met him, anyway. But then, I guess he could have been nice because you had a gun aimed at him."

"A gun wouldn't scare Nick."

"I'm glad you have him out there with you,

then," Beth said. She let go of Sarah and turned back to the desk.

Sarah realized how blessed she was to have been assigned Nick as her FTO, in all aspects.

"I'll be better once he's caught. I'll think about what you said," Beth promised as she started closing down the computer. She had several Internet browsers open, with many small message boxes on screen. She'd apparently been talking to some friends online.

That's what Sarah had thought all along, but Beth didn't need to hear 'I told you so' from her. "I know, hon. We'll all feel better then." She pulled her sister's hand away from the computer mouse. "I need to use this now. Just leave it as is, okay?"

"Let me close out this stuff for you."

Sarah dared not venture into law-enforcement-officer mode. Nor another oldest-sister lecture. She'd laid it on thick enough for one night. "I can do it later. One quick shortcut and it'll all shut down at once. Let me just check my e-mails."

Beth nodded. "Okay." They were both silent, watching the hourglass on her computer turn.

Sarah slipped into the chair and stopped the process so she could search for clues as to who her sister had been talking to. "I'm going to go look at the condo again tomorrow afternoon, take some measurements and figure out where to put things. Why don't you come with me?"

"Yeah, maybe I will. I'm going to bed now. Thanks for the advice, Sarah."

"Anytime," she said, anxious to start her investigation.

FOURTEEN

Nick left for work early again the next evening. In almost the same spot that he'd come across the stranded woman, he found a young boy trying to carry an injured dog. Nick never could turn away from a child in need. He called the parents and waited for them to come get the boy and the dog.

By the time he arrived at the precinct, his trainee was once again out on duty.

"Matthews, be sure to study the list we put in your box. We'll have extra officers on the midway, but most are going to be in street clothes. I don't want a repeat of last night," the shift supervisor said as he headed into his office. "Meet me back here after you're in uniform. I'll take you downtown, since all the patrol cars are on the streets tonight."

After studying the list of officers and their assignments, Nick dressed and hurried back to meet the supervisor. They were headed out his office door when the phone on his desk rang. At the same time, dispatch radioed in. "Sorry, Lieutenant, this caller wanted to talk to you. I think it's the rapist. He sounds very creepy."

The supervisor turned off his radio and pressed speakerphone. "Lieutenant Douglas. Who is this?"

"Telling you that would ruin all the fun, wouldn't it?" the caller replied.

"You're having fun?" Douglas tapped the eraser of his pencil on the desk.

"Oh yeah," the man growled. "I never knew the pursuit could be better than the catch. So you can move her as much as you like, but I'll find her," he said in a raspy, forced voice.

The lieutenant grimaced, twirling the pencil from finger to finger. "Who are you looking for?"

Nick rested his hands on the desk and closed his eyes, praying it wasn't Beth. Praying he wouldn't know her name.

"Don't play dumb with me."

The suspect was in a busy place, with lots of background noises. Nick listened for something distinctive. A whistle. Water. Anything they could use to track him.

"Oh, I forgot, you're a smart criminal, right? That's why you have to resort to forcing yourself on women…."

That obviously ticked the caller off. He was breathing hard now. Suddenly, the background noises became muffled. Was he in a closed-in area? A mall? Nick picked up a sound he'd heard before—the rhythmic clack of metal and the hum of electric generators.

"Oh, they pretend to be waiting, pretend to be pure…."

Nick wanted to reach out and grab the man through the phone. *Come on, creep, you're not as clever as you think.*

The lieutenant took his time responding. They had to keep him on the line as long as possible, to give them more details to go on when studying the recording. "We didn't move anyone. Why don't you tell me why you're taking your anger out on innocent women?"

The caller chuckled, a deep and sinister laugh. "It's your job to figure that out. Mine is to find her before you find me. I'm hiding in plain sight."

Nick heard the music from the Ferris wheel at the Harvest Festival just then, behind the caller's voice. Immediately, he ran out the door, heading to his own car, and grabbing for his radio as he did so. "Officer 235 en route to Harvest Festival. Officer 318, code 33, contact by phone."

He was racing downtown a minute later when his phone rang. "Nick, what's going on?" Sarah asked.

"The rapist called from a pay phone at the

carnival. I could hear the Ferris wheel. Where are you?" He pulled up to the first traffic barricade and waved himself past the security guards. He realized as he got out of his car that he could hear the Ferris wheel music for blocks. The suspect could be anywhere.

They'd had more problems with gangs in the downtown area lately, and Nick was thankful there were more officers on duty tonight.

"I'm near the chicken hut—" Sarah said quietly. The same music was playing in the background.

"I'll be right there," he interrupted, and disconnected. He tried to look casual as he searched for Sarah, but panic was taking over. In the crowds of pedestrians, he spotted the blonde baker they'd met in the alley the night before. Maybe she'd seen his partner.

"Hi, Officer Matthews," she said, handing him a coupon for a discount on a costume rental. "Need a costume?"

He eyed someone dressed as a big yellow bird walking past the chicken hut. "No thanks, I brought my own. Looks like you've already drummed up some business." He nodded. "Is that one of your costumes?"

"Yes, interest has been even better than I expected…."

Nick thought of the muffled sounds during the

rapist's phone call. A close-fitting mask could do that…. He didn't have time for small talk, not with a predator on the loose. "Good, have a nice evening."

I know you're short, Sarah, but where are you?

The yellow bird was pacing back and forth in front of a bar overflowing with young customers, as if it was ready to pounce.

Was their suspect in costume?

The bird took a few steps, just as Nick heard Sarah say over the radio, "Suspicious party in front of the leaning…"

Suddenly, the bird took off running.

Someone yelled, but Nick couldn't make out what was said. Seconds later the yellow-feathered creature pushed through a crowd, then ran into a man and woman, knocking the woman down. A large pink purse went flying.

Nick raced forward, dodging people and baby strollers, as screams erupted.

The man kicked the chicken, then took off, after pausing a second to look at his date on the ground.

What was going on? Was he waiting for the girl, or wanting the purse? Nick wasn't sure who was after whom, or what was going down. He was closing the gap as the college-age female rolled over and shoved the bird away.

The bird struggled back to its feet, the bulky costume adding to its problems. It took one step toward the man then stopped as the suspect disappeared between two buildings. The bird knelt in front of the upset woman.

Nick yanked the costumed figure aside with one hand and helped the girl to her feet with the other. Neither the bird or the woman reached for the purse lying on the sidewalk.

Nick confirmed that the victim was okay, and instructed her to stay close while he sorted things out. Then he turned to the bird, which was stomping its feet, struggling to get away, as other police officers pushed through the gathering crowd.

"I had him, Matthews!"

Nick let the yellow feathers drop from his hand.

Sarah?

FIFTEEN

She was still reading Nick the riot act as yet another officer approached, pushing the crowd back. "He advertised to meet interested parties here, Matthews…." she mumbled, nodding toward the hysterical woman.

"I'll talk to you in a minute," he growled. He picked up the giant pink purse and slid it onto his shoulder. *What the blazes is she carrying in here?*

Nick looked at Sarah, confused. He pulled her away from the victim, as he would have separated the individuals in any fight, then scanned the crowd once more, looking for the suspect. All he saw was a woman arguing with one of their plainclothes officers. It seemed as if he'd missed catching the real suspect, for an undercover cop.

"Didn't Lieutenant Douglas tell you?" Sarah whispered.

Nick looked around the scene, assessing the

situation. Crowd of people, gangbangers lurking in the distance. They probably weren't an issue. "Tell me what?"

"About my disguise."

"He didn't. And just in case the suspect is still hanging around, you're being treated just like our other suspects. We don't dare let on that we have cops in costumes out here. How many others are there?"

"Just me," she muttered, as Nick pushed her up to the wall of the bar and made a show of frisking her.

"This is a family event. You should be ashamed of yourself," he said, loud enough for the gawkers to hear. Then he added under his breath, "I can't believe Douglas failed to tell me something this critical." He gave her the once-over as he turned her around. "The suspect called. Douglas was talking to him. I didn't know you'd be…a chicken. It wasn't on the list."

"Give her the stupid purse, then," Sarah yelled. "Let me go."

"You're under arrest for robbery," he said, pulling a set of handcuffs from his belt.

"You're kidding me," she growled.

"Everyone break it up," Nick bellowed. "Go on your way. We have this situation under control." He turned her around, just then noticing several gang members moving closer.

"What's going on?" Sarah whispered.

Nick hated to cuff his backup, but put the cuffs very loosely on his undercover partner before handing the purse to the young woman. "I'm not positive, but it doesn't look good. Don't break your cover unless it's absolutely imperative, Roberts."

A witness started swearing at Nick. "That's my purse! This *stupid duck* knocked it out of my hand."

"I'm not a duck," Sarah retorted, leaning forward and playing along with the arrest. She'd learned the first week of FBI training that undercover work was the most dangerous assignment of all. Things could change at a moment's notice. They'd never given her the chance to prove herself because of her size. This was her chance to do so here. "Don't you know the difference between a duck bill and a chicken beak, you moron? This is a beak!" She started clucking like a chicken, startling the crowd.

Nick grabbed her by the wing and tugged her close to the coed in the miniskirt.

"Give me my purse back," the tough-looking woman said, pushing her way through the crowd. She belonged to a gang, Sarah suddenly realized as she peered through the feathers hanging in front of her eyeholes.

The crowd was thinning, but the gang members remained, swarming around them. The woman yelled, "You're no better than that thief, pig. Give me the purse, and they'll back off."

Without another word, Nick pulled the hefty woman's arms behind her back. He pulled out a second set of handcuffs and radioed for backup. "That's threatening an officer, not to mention what we may find when we open this bag to verify its ownership. And I'm sure your customers are anxious to make a buy…. You've saved us a lot of work, gathering them all together for us…."

Sarah watched in amazement at how quickly the crowd dispersed. At how Nick had taken control of the situation, without revealing that they had under-cover officers on duty, mixed in with the throngs around them.

She'd been so intent on the suspect she'd totally missed that the purse was far too fat to contain the average college girl's supply of makeup and sundries. Sarah eyed the frightened all-American coed, clean-cut, except for her miniskirt, then the hefty gang member wearing tons of makeup. Even if the monstrous purse wasn't filled with drugs, it made no sense for the student to be traveling with it.

Besides, pink clashed with her outfit. The coed seemed the type to coordinate every detail.

The other officers were milling through the crowd, some in street clothes, a handful in uniform. They all knew Sarah's identity.

"The bird's under arrest for robbery," Nick told Jared Daniels as he came to assist. "I've searched her, but leave the costume on, let her sweat a little."

She knew he was trying to tell the others to keep up the charade.

"I read you. Good job, Sergeant," Jared Daniels said with a smile.

Sarah thought of how close they'd come to initiating a gang riot, and her heart raced. Give her the cold, calculated threat of a terrorist and she was in her zone, but here in the midst of gang members she was as green as they came.

"Where's the squad car?" Nick asked her in a whisper.

"I drove my own car," she answered quietly. "Kinda blows the cover to have a police escort to a party."

Jeremy Logan stepped through the crowd and handed Nick a set of keys. "My car's at the end of the block. Take the bird and the victim, and I'll have Daniels bring the owner of the purse in for you."

Nick looked at Jared and leaned close. "Get those cuffs back to me. They're my grandfather's."

"Will do," Jared confirmed, then led the gang member in the opposite direction.

Nick escorted Sarah to the car, the coed—the rapist's target—alongside. Lieutenant Douglas met them at the vehicle. "We almost had him, but good job, both of you," he said in a low voice. "Get back on the streets ASAP. We'll talk about this later. I expect to make sure the teardown of the festival goes smoothly, so plan to stay late to talk with me about the call."

Sarah took a deep breath, thankful that she could hide behind the chicken head for the moment. She'd blown it big this time.

SIXTEEN

After Nick put both women into the backseat, he briefly explained to the victim that Sarah was not a purse snatcher, but an undercover cop, and had recognized her date.

"Do you know the man you were having a drink with?" Sarah asked.

"No, I'd just met him," she said quietly. "Why? What did he do?"

"We're not at liberty to say. But we're going to ask you to talk with the detective working this case."

Sarah closed her eyes and realized it was going to be a very long night. She was certain she recognized this girl from Coedspace, but couldn't recall if she'd listed Waiting for Marriage as one of her social groups. Despite Nick trying to put the cuffs on loosely, the steel cut into her thumb as she tried to move. Not only that, her cheek hurt from the suspect kicking her.

As soon as he opened the back door of the car at

the station she climbed out and turned her back to him. "Get these off me."

"Sorry I had to do that," he said gently, and her heart melted. "You okay?"

"Yeah, I'll be fine. I need some ice for my cheek. I'll go get some from the lounge."

"The detectives are going to talk to her. Meet me in observation room four right away."

Nick and Sarah listened in as Wang and a female detective questioned the coed. Pretty soon, Wang brought a laptop into the interview room. He had her sit down at the computer and show him where the suspect had contacted her.

Between tears and sobs, the young woman led them to the Coedspace site.

"Yes, thank you!" Sarah mumbled, glad of the soundproof walls in the room. "That's it! I knew it! Every one of the sexual assault victims has personal information posted on this site." She jotted a note to deliver to the detective. "I'm going to have him ask if she's involved with the Waiting for Marriage group." She stepped out of the room to do so, and a minute later was back.

Nick nodded at her. "How'd you know that?"

"Know what?"

"The caller said 'they pretend to be waiting, pretend to be pure.' I think you're right, he's targeting the abstinence members."

They waited for the detective to ask the question. The victim scrolled down, searching frantically for the guy she'd planned to meet. "His picture was on here. It's gone now. He was part of the Waiting for Marriage chapter. He seemed so nice online…."

Sarah felt the blood drain from her face, and the ice pack she held sent a wave of cold through her veins. She and Nick listened as the detectives went through everything the girl remembered about the man, from their online conversations to their meeting.

"What was his screen name?" the computer expert asked.

The coed turned red. "BadBoynomor. He said he's reformed from his bad boy days. I met him through a chat that the abstinence group held last week."

Sarah got on the phone, relieved when her father answered. "Dad, is everything okay there?"

"Fine, what's up?"

"We have another lead, but I need Beth's membership list for her Waiting for Marriage chapter."

"We just packed her paperwork. The Realtor called and said we can start moving tomorrow, so I went over and finished packing up her old house."

Sarah couldn't even think about the move right now. "Sorry to make you unpack, but this is really important. Call me when you find it." She hesitated, then added, "Oh, and I'll probably be home a little late, so don't worry about me. I have more paperwork than usual tonight."

She rolled her eyes when her dad told her to call and he'd be waiting outside when she got home. Did he really expect her to do that? She was a police officer.

She said goodbye, then met with the department artist to come up with a sketch of the man she'd tried to bring in.

Nick handed her a fresh ice pack. "So how did you come up with the abstinence link?"

"After work last night, I logged on to check my e-mail. Beth had been using the computer, and I told her to leave all her windows open, that I'd close them down. I noticed several conversations she was having with girls from the group. All of a sudden, someone sent an instant message, and it was clear they thought I was Beth. She hadn't logged off the main chat room, apparently."

"And?"

"I had a hunch," Sarah said vaguely.

Nick looked at her suspiciously. "That's it?"

She nodded.

The artist, M. J. Daniels, arrived and introduced herself while she got her supplies from a cupboard. "Hi, Nick," she added with a smile.

He greeted her and asked about her new grandson. He and M.J. had obviously known each other's families for a while.

While they visited, Sarah tried to erase the drawing from Beth's neighbor's rape from her memory. It was difficult. This suspect matched too closely.

M.J. started asking questions, and she tried to answer as accurately as possible. "The last victim had him portrayed so well, it's difficult to think if there was anything different," Sarah said at last.

"Close your eyes, Officer Roberts," Nick suggested. "Concentrate on his face. Nothing else."

She followed his instructions, but listening to the deep timbre of his voice was killing her concentration. All she could see was the shock on her partner's face when he'd realized *she* was the chicken. The way Nick said her name had changed, too.

In her mind, he had become not her training officer, but the man who had held her at her sister's house. The man who had comforted her. Supported her. The man she wanted to fall in love with.

"What d'ya see?" Nick said gruffly. "Come on, Roberts, we need to get back out there and get this guy."

Tonight he was the angry partner with trust issues again.

He'd changed in the last week. It seemed as if he'd been trusting her, been interested in her, but now she'd broken that trust. And it would be that much harder to rebuild. Tears stung her eyes.

"Go work on the report, Sergeant Matthews," she said finally, her eyes still closed. "I'm close to having him in my head again," she lied.

"I'll stay and help—" he offered, but Sarah cut him off.

"Just go. I'll get it done." She set the ice pack on the table.

"Go ahead, Nick," the artist said in her gentle voice. "I'm used to this."

He gave a sigh of disgust, and his chair scraped the floor as he stood. "I'll be in the report room," he stated, then left.

Sarah felt her skin heating again, and fought for control. She reached for the ice pack, hoping it would hide the flush on her face. The last thing she needed was for the police artist to turn her in for having a crush on her training officer. Sarah took a shallow breath, trying to calm her racing heart. *Focus on the face. The suspect's face.* She tried again.

Deep breath. Inhale. Exhale. Visualize... *No, not Nick's face!*

It was useless. She jumped from the chair and paced around the artist's office. "I can't get the last victim's picture out of my mind."

The middle-aged woman smiled. "Funny, I was

seeing Nick. It happens to his witnesses quite often," she added. "There must be something about that voice of his," she said dreamily. "But don't let him intimidate you."

Sarah stared at her as if the woman had been reading her mind. "Is it hot in here?" She unbuttoned the costume at the neck and tried to tug it away from her skin.

"Don't worry. You'll get over him. They all do, apparently. I mean, he's not married. He must have some awful trait that scares women away."

Sarah felt the tension ebb. "Yeah, he's a cop. Who'd want to marry one of us?"

"There you go." M.J. said with a laugh. "Come on, I'll walk you through it again. I can guarantee my voice won't be a distraction."

"Thank you," she said as she settled across the table from the woman, a smile still on her face.

"You're at the carnival. What's it like?" M.J. asked casually.

Sarah took a deep breath and closed her eyes. "I smell fried chicken, cotton candy…liquor…marijuana…." She imagined her phone ringing, but refused to answer it. Even in her mind, Nick Matthews was a distraction. "I looked around for someone fitting the description given by the last victim. I had to brush the feathers out of my face. Then I saw him nuzzled up to the girl in the miniskirt."

Sarah paused. "In her picture on the Web site she was in a miniskirt, and I figured maybe she'd told him she'd be wearing one. I looked back at him, made the decision to approach…to bring him in for questioning."

"So you determined that he matched the factors you were looking for. What shape was his face?"

"Square…Caucasian…thick eyebrows…" She continued until they had a sketch. When it was complete, she gave her approval and got up to go, only to find Nick waiting at the door.

Despite M.J.'s promise that Sarah would get over him, her pulse went crazy again.

SEVENTEEN

"I'm going to change out of this costume and I'll be ready to get back on patrol in a couple of minutes," Sarah said, running down the hall before he could say a word. He smiled at the confident way she carried herself, even when dressed in a wacky chicken costume.

"Good. I'll wait in the lounge," he said warily. The puffiness on her cheek was gone, he noted, but the skin was starting to bruise.

Nick eyed M.J., who turned her back and started working on her computer.

Something was going on.

"Did things turn out okay?" he asked.

She held up the sketch. "Perfectly."

"What's her problem?"

"She's your partner. You need to ask her, Sergeant Matthews."

"Don't 'Sergeant Matthews' me…."

"I'm not your aunt in here, Nicky. Your presence was a distraction. I knew I could get what we needed without you, that's all. Let me scan this in, and you can make copies."

"What's that supposed to mean?"

"It means you need to get over your own issues, Nick. Not everyone is out to double-cross you, not everyone is… Never mind. Go talk to Sarah. It's none of my business."

He thought of pushing, but knew the situation would only get more complicated. It was probably obvious to M.J. how he felt about Sarah. He'd never been a good actor.

Nick waited in the officers lounge, more puzzled than he had been before. It was totally like his aunt to shoot it at him straight, with both barrels if need be. It wasn't like her to claim anything wasn't her business….

When Sarah came out of the locker room, he handed her the keys to the police cruiser. "You certain you're up to finishing the shift tonight?"

"I'm okay. It's not my first black eye, and I'm sure it won't be my last."

"Let me look."

"It's fine." She turned her head, trying to keep him from seeing. But he gently lifted her chin and turned the injured area to the light. "How bad does it hurt?"

"I've had worse in training. I'm good to go get this creep."

"I'll just bet you are." He paused, still holding her chin. "So what was the problem in there?"

She pulled away and walked out of the station into the darkness. "I told you, I…" As her voice faded away, he followed.

Out in the parking yard he couldn't see her face as clearly, but at least they were out of range of anyone seeing or overhearing them. If she said what he hoped she would, privacy would be a definite plus. She couldn't hide forever.

"I had to have some time to replay what happened out there, before you showed up—when I was watching the guy. I couldn't concentrate with you breathing down my neck."

Why hadn't his aunt said that? "I'm tired of being left in the dark, Roberts," he grumbled. "Trust goes both ways."

She turned toward him and nodded. "I'm glad you realize that, Nick," she said. "Pardon me, Sergeant Matthews." She ducked quickly into the cruiser and started the engine.

"What's that supposed to mean?" he asked as he got in the passenger's side.

"It means I don't need a guardian every minute. I know what I can and can't do, on and off the job. Whose toes I can and can't step on." She pulled out of the parking lot onto the street, radioing dispatch of their available status.

"It's good to hear that. So what's with going out there undercover without telling me?" He stared at her.

"I didn't tell you my idea last night, Sergeant, because I didn't think the commander would approve it," she said. "He said he'd fill you in when you showed up at the station."

"And he probably would have, had our suspect not called. You should have mentioned it when I phoned to get your location." Nick was not ready for six more hours in the same car with the woman who was quickly capturing his heart.

"I was too close to the suspect to reveal my status."

He stared straight ahead. "You can say that again. You're too close to this case to be pushing, period, Roberts. It was one thing when another case led to evidence on your sister's...."

"That wasn't what I was saying." She turned onto University Avenue to patrol their usual route, then radioed dispatch once again, to find out who else had been covering the area.

While they waited for a response, Nick let her have it. "No? Well, maybe it's what you should have been saying. Or maybe you'd like to go back to explaining why I was sent out of the room when you—"

"I'm not thinking about what I'd like, Sergeant. I'm trying not to step on your toes."

Twenty minutes of silence was broken by a call from dispatch.

"Officer 318, suspicious activity at McKinley Elementary School. Possible fireworks being set off."

Sarah glanced down at the computer keyboard and pulled the radio mike from the clip on the dash. "Copy. En route. Who is the reporting party?"

"It was a concerned driver," the dispatcher said. "The name is on the file."

Sarah needed to change lanes to make the next turn, and didn't have an opening. She switched on the red and blue lights and slowed down to cut behind the pickup next to her. "Traffic's heavy at the moment. Would you look it up?"

Nick turned the car-mount so he could read the computer. Just then a name popped up on their report: M. J. Daniels. His aunt. What was she up to now?

He covered his brow with his hand and shook his head. *Doggone it, M.J. I don't need your help. Especially not now.*

"Any details of what we're looking for?" Sarah asked. "Inside or outside the school?"

"Negative, just suspicious lights and popping sounds," dispatch relayed before Nick could skim the report.

"Suspicious lights, great," she said, and turned off University Avenue. "Sergeant Matthews? Everything okay? Was there a name of a contact?"

"It was M.J., so I'm sure it's legit. It's probably a reflection or something, but we should check it out. We never know until we look."

She cut the flashing lights, turned onto McKinley Street and drove around the perimeter of the school yard. The second time around she said, "I don't see anything, do you?"

"No," he said quietly, not sure how to explain his aunt to her.

Sarah pulled into the next parking lot and radioed that they'd be out of the vehicle. "Do you smell any evidence of fireworks? Exactly what are suspicious lights going to look like? I mean, it's not as if a prankster made the call, right?" she asked, a sarcastic tone to her voice. She walked several yards, the heavy, clublike flashlight in her hand, then stopped and stared at the main entrance.

For a minute, he thought she'd actually seen something. Then she turned and crossed her arms over her chest.

"Did you two set this up? There's nothing here."

"No." He shook his head. *Trust works both ways.* "I had nothing to do with it, but with M.J...."

"What did she tell you?"

"She's my aunt, Sarah."

She stared at him, working her jaw, pressing her lips together. "That's par for the course, isn't it? Is there anyone else on the force I should watch out for?" she asked, clearly annoyed, but understandably so. He'd expected her to explode.

"You've probably already met both of my brothers, Kent and Garrett. Jared Daniels is my cousin. That's all. Let's check the doors of the building, take a walk and make sure she wasn't calling in a legitimate concern. We need to clear the air, Sarah."

He could see panic on her face. She turned back toward the car, and he reached out and stopped her.

"I want to know what really happened back there with M.J. For the record, she told me to talk to you and to deal with my own issues. I'm guessing that's what this bogus call is about." He stepped over, tested the front doors of the school, then walked beside her, circling the building. "So what was the problem?"

Sarah glanced at him, her left eyebrow arched, as if she was trying to look innocent. "You don't need to know," she said firmly.

Dispatch radioed for an ambulance to treat a bar fight at the Harvest Festival, and Nick turned his radio down. "I get the distinct feeling that I'm the only one in the dark on this. My aunt tells me I need to deal with my own issues, which is probably true. It's a challenge just walking through those doors most days, but I'm doing my best. So what have I done wrong?"

"This is one time you'd probably rather be in the dark…."

"In case you haven't figured one thing out about me yet, Sarah, I don't give up, no matter how great the odds against me." They came to the handicapped entrance. Nick pressed the automated button and the door clattered as if it was going to open.

Sarah dropped her flashlight and drew her gun.

"Whoa. I was just testing to see if it was locked. It's okay." Nick fought the urge to smile.

He didn't dare.

She relaxed, lowering the Glock to her side.

"Sorry. I really didn't mean to…"

"Test my reactions?" She put the gun into her holster and picked up the flashlight. "Afraid I'm getting sluggish?"

Nick was more afraid of her than she realized. Of what he was feeling for her. Of what she wanted from him. And why his aunt had sent them out here on a wild-goose chase. "That's the last of my worries, Roberts." He waited, challenging her to pick up their conversation where it had left off. "Why are you afraid of telling me what happened in there?"

"Trust me, Sergeant. I'm not afraid. But you don't want to know. Especially not now. Probably not ever."

He took a step closer and looked into her big brown eyes. "If you weren't my trainee, would this be an issue?" He needed to know if he was right.

"But I *am,* Nick." She spoke gently. "Until this phase of my training is over, this conversation should not be taking place." This time she didn't correct herself. "I'm not even sure how soon after this phase we could have this conversation, but I told you from the very beginning, I'm not going to do anything to hurt you or your career. And I mean that." She walked around him, proceeded to the next entrance of the school and checked it. "So let's finish this call and get back out on the streets."

He wanted to kiss her, right here and now, but knew better than to do something so stupid. "Tell me what happened, Sarah...."

She kept walking toward the next entrance, but finally turned and met his eyes without flinching. "I couldn't get you out of my head. And every time you said something, it got worse. There, are you happy?"

"That's it?"

"It's kind of a problem when every time I tried to describe the suspect, all I could see in my mind was how mad you were when you discovered I was the chicken...." She shook her head. "I'm sorry I made a mess of everything."

He moved closer and touched her bruised cheek gently. "I was mad because I was worried about you, Sarah. I didn't used to understand why they have the rule that couples can't serve on the same shift. After tonight, I get it. It's next to impossible to focus on the job when your partner is in jeopardy. Until you came along, I didn't think it could get any worse than defending another officer. It can."

She turned her head and briefly pressed her lips to his fingers. "I know. I don't want to hurt you, Nick. I'm so grateful that God provided this chance for me to get to know you, but it's come with a huge price tag. I should have told you about my suspicions, but I'm not allowed to call you off duty during training. I—"

"You might have had him if I hadn't shown up at the wrong time. But we're a step closer than we were twelve hours ago. If things stay quiet tonight, we'll head in early and talk to Lieutenant Douglas."

"Your *aunt* could tell there's something happening between us, Nick. How are we ever going to keep it from our supervisor?"

"Knowing M.J., she was probably hoping to play matchmaker, more than having any real evidence."

"I don't know, Nick. I must have been as transparent as glass. She assured me I'd get over you like they all do."

"What 'all' was she talking about?"

Sarah shrugged. "She said you must have some awful trait that scares women away." He heard the challenge in her voice. She was competitive, and not afraid to take anyone on. Not even a man a foot taller and at least a hundred pounds heavier.

He crossed his arms over his chest. "Yeah? Did you take her seriously?"

Sarah's lip twitched. "I believe I laughed and claimed no one wants to marry a cop. Seems to be my experience, anyway."

Nick laughed in turn. "Right now, I think that's pretty lucky for me. Either that, or God's been working overtime to get us here." He widened his stance, as if to keep her from pushing him away. "So do you really think you'd want to marry a cop?" His voice was painfully calm, his gaze steady. He didn't realize until he'd spoken, that she could ask him the same question. He'd never dated a female officer. He wondered if it could work. Would he be able to handle her putting her life on the line if he didn't see her in action? If they weren't there to back each other up?

"Don't even go there," she declared, obviously unaware of how ardent her voice sounded.

"I'd like to talk to the training supervisor, see if he could get you assigned to someone else, just to stay on the straight and narrow with the higher ups."

"It's two more weeks, Nick. With four-day work weeks, that's only eight more days that you're my trainer. We'll have this conversation after that. Please don't risk your career." She looked into his eyes, and in the moonlight he could see fear in her own. "What if what we're feeling is a reaction to going through some stressful calls together?"

"Is that what you think? Because I don't."

Her eyes grew moist, and she shook her head. "I've had a crush on you since high school, Nick, so I've loved getting to know you these last few weeks. But—"

"That's a little creepy," he said with a smile. "Because I had a crush on you, too. I was scared to death to ask you out, being I was just a lowly sophomore and you were a brainiac senior."

"I hope that's a compliment."

"Oh yeah. Cute and brains, perfect combination."

Her face turned pink and she bit her lower lip nervously. "That's so strange. Fourteen years later, and here we are, finally getting to know each other."

"Then why are you afraid that it can't work out?" he asked, touching her arm. "Wouldn't it be worth finding out?"

"I'm terrified that you'd risk harming your career over me, and resent me because of it."

He didn't know how to respond. What she said made sense, so why was it impossible to think of going along with her plan?

"I don't know how this department works with officer relationships," she added, "but even if we decide to see each other after I'm done with my training, it would be wise to keep things pretty quiet for a while, wouldn't it?"

"How long is a while? Because I'm getting on in years…."

"Thanks a bunch. *I'm* older than you," she said with a smile.

"Seriously, Sarah, how do you ever downplay the dishonored cop and the former FBI agent who were FTO and trainee? It's always going to be there to cast a shadow. If I—"

Sarah backed away. "No," she said, trying to sound sure of herself. "There's plenty of time to see how it goes, Nick. There's no need for either of us to jeopardize our careers before we even get them back. Right?"

EIGHTEEN

Dispatch interrupted Nick's answer, asking for a status check. Though the call was routine, the timing couldn't have been worse. Or better. He knew Sarah was right.

A year ago, he'd have had no problem letting a couple of weeks go by. Now, his world was different. He was different.

Nick wasn't much concerned about having to hold off asking her out on a date. He was *very* worried about both of them keeping their personal feelings from affecting their jobs. He remembered how difficult it had been when he'd been distracted with his sister. But when he'd seen Sarah undercover, he'd nearly lost it.

Could he really get emotionally involved with a woman whose life was constantly at risk every day she went to work?

"Three-eighteen clear," she said. "Returning to service."

"Two thirty-five clear," he echoed.

Sarah's father called as they were heading back to the squad car.

"They couldn't find the membership list," she told Nick after they'd spoken. "The only other copy Beth has is on her flash drive, which she can't locate. She thinks it's packed in one of the boxes at her house."

"We can run by and take a look," he suggested. "We really need to see the list of members so the experts can start profiling the suspect. While you drive, I'll call Douglas, let him know what's going on."

She made a beeline for the cruiser, walking in silence. "I'm sorry I told you, Sergeant Matthews," she said, just before she got inside and closed the door.

Nick said a quick prayer before joining her. "I don't have any regrets, Sarah." Many questions. Countless concerns. Not enough answers. "It gives us something to look forward to when you're through training with me. And hopefully, this case will be solved soon, so we don't have to be partners. I've gotta be honest, I still believe it's best to tell the supervisor, but not today. I need some time to think it all through. Could I call you this afternoon?"

"You can, but we're going to be moving, so I'm not sure when would be the best time to talk."

"That's okay. I might just happen by my sister's condo about that time, and see if I can lend a hand."

"You don't have to do that," Sarah said, though she was smiling from ear to ear. "But you'd sure win some points with my dad, just in case you and I work this out. And if you don't happen to get along with him, you can run fast."

Nick laughed. He realized it had been a long time since he had simply laughed. M.J. was right; he did need to get over his trust issues. If he didn't, he'd miss a lot of happiness. He had to take a chance on someone sometime. Why not now? He couldn't think of a woman who had changed his life more in such a short time.

"So we're looking for an itty-bitty flash drive, huh?"

"And you thought your detective days were over," she said as they drove to the west side of the university. "Beth is going to miss being so close to work."

"Sometimes it's nice to have a few minutes in the car to think things through and clear your head when the day's over." Nick reached for the radio and called in their location.

Lieutenant Douglas answered. "Copy that. Will meet you there."

Nick looked at Sarah.

"Are you ready?" she asked.

"Ready or not, we'll see where we stand after this."

The two cars pulled up to the house at the same

time. Sarah explained to the supervisor how she'd come to her conclusion that the suspect's motive was linked to rejection from some woman in his life. "He sent that message with my sister's neighbor, and used the word *prude* to describe her. Nick mentioned the rapist's comment today. I think he's either a member of the group, or someone in the group rejected him. Now he's out for revenge."

"I thought you'd made the connection to the Coedspace Web site?"

"Coedspace has chat rooms for every interest group and organization under the stars, Lieutenant. After my sister got off my computer the other night, I got on. People see you're on and start a conversation. The girl from the festival tonight said our guy's screen name is BadBoynomor. If we get a list of local members, the investigators can find him. My sister is one of the abstinence group organizers, and they're hosting a state-wide conference here next weekend."

The supervisor swore under his breath. "When did you plan on sharing this information, Roberts?"

"Sergeant Matthews and I just put the pieces together, Lieutenant." She eyed Nick, wondering if he *wanted* half the credit.

"Let's find this list, and we'll talk about your involvement when the case is over."

They walked up the front steps together, discussing the incident at the festival.

Sarah put the key in the door and turned it, noticing at once that the click of the dead bolt was missing. She turned the key back, realizing the door hadn't been locked. She put her finger to her lips. "My family wouldn't leave the house unlocked," she whispered.

Nick pointed to himself and held up one finger, pointed to Sarah and held up two, then indicated the lieutenant would enter third.

Her gun in one hand, Sarah quietly turned the knob with the other and forced the door open with her boot. Nick slipped past her, waited as she entered, then the lieutenant came in behind them.

Boxes were scattered haphazardly around the room. Many were tipped on their side, as if there'd been a struggle. "They stacked the boxes in the dining room," Sarah whispered. "Someone's been here since they left."

The lieutenant pulled his Glock, directing Nick to search the upstairs and Sarah to stay on guard while he checked the kitchen.

She had a bad feeling as she inched toward the front window and peeked out. There were too many shadows to see any details. Someone could be out there, watching, waiting. Whoever had done this would be crazy to stay with two cop cars on site, but she knew all too well that serial criminals enjoyed watching their crimes being discovered. It gave them power. Fed their ego to think they'd gotten away with something.

"The back door is broken in," Lieutenant Douglas said as he rejoined her. "You're not going to stay on street patrol long, Roberts."

"Lieutenant, get up here," Nick yelled from upstairs. "Roberts, stay put...."

Sarah was right behind the shift commander. She found the attic loft a shambles. Her sister's bed had been shredded—

Nick blocked her view and pushed her into the hallway. "You gotta back off, Roberts. Don't touch anything."

"It's torn apart," she said, staring at him. Fear and anger raged in his deep gray eyes. "What's wrong, Nick? What else did he do?" She struggled to see into the room. "Did he leave a threat or something?"

"Trust me, Sarah," he whispered. "Stay out here for a few minutes or go downstairs." He held her firmly. "Yes, he's made one heck of a statement this time...."

From the hallway, she heard the lieutenant talking to the dispatcher. "We need a homicide investigator."

Sarah pushed, trying to get past Nick. "Who is it?"

He shrugged. "I was just going to look for an I.D. when you came up here. It's not Beth. Are you sure she didn't have someone else living with her?"

"No. Not that I knew of."

Just then, they heard a deep gasp.

"He's alive!" the supervisor yelled. "Get an ambulance here now! I need help to stop the bleeding."

NINETEEN

For two hours doctors operated on Beth's fiancé, hoping to save his life. Now they were in wait-and-see mode. Sarah couldn't get the image of the body on her sister's floor out of her head.

She and Nick had been covered with blood, as was Lieutenant Douglas. Since it was a family-related case, Sarah had been released from duty. Nick stayed on. The crime scene investigators moved all of the boxes out of the house after they'd taken pictures, hoping that, in the struggle, the suspect had left some kind of evidence.

Another officer escorted Sarah home, where she broke the news to her parents, so they could help tell her sister. She'd cleaned up and changed out of uniform before they went to the hospital to check on Steve.

After the surgery, the doctor met Beth and Steve's parents in the lobby. "The knife did a lot of damage, but I think we've been able to stop all of the bleeders. He's going to be lucky to survive this."

"Can I see him yet?" Beth asked.

"In a while, after he's more stable."

Sarah felt numb as she witnessed the pain her sister was going through. Her parents were doting on the baby of the family, as they had been for the last week.

Sarah leaned her head back against the wall and felt her eyes drifting closed. She hadn't slept well in weeks. It was bound to catch up with her sooner or later….

Lieutenant Douglas's words echoed in her head: *You won't be on the street patrol long.* She'd been so focused on the case that she'd probably ruined her chances of staying on at the Fossil Creek Police Department….

She woke a few minutes later to find tears streaming down her face. Sarah wiped her face, then excused herself and found the hospital chapel. She needed time to talk to God one-on-one. Sitting in the pew, she stared at the cross.

She knew that God understood the pain of betrayal, the agony of disappointment, the bruises of failure. Her pain was nothing Jesus hadn't suffered over and again. Yet he went on.

She folded her hands together, forming a cushion on the pew back ahead. Resting her forehead on them, she closed her eyes.

I don't even know how to pray, God. I want the impossible. I want Steve to heal completely. I want there to be no scars, no reminders of tonight. I want my sister to heal, and one day be able to forget all of this. But I know You have a greater purpose for her. I know that in my heart, but it's so hard to watch my little sister make her way through this pain.

Forgive me for being so worried about my own job security that I held back from passing my suspicions along. Forgive me for being so concerned about trying to make everything go my own way. When will I learn how to juggle all of these pieces of my life? I'm thirty-four years old and I still have no idea where You want me, or what You want me to do. What I thought I was good at, I keep messing up.

I really botched things up tonight, God. Help me to do the right thing for Nick. He shouldn't have to be punished for my mistakes. Help me to make things right. Help me to do the honorable thing, even if it means I lose Nick.

She felt the tears threatening to take control.

I can't even seem to get the timing right on falling in love. It had taken her fourteen years to catch Nick Matthews's attention, and now, in one night, she'd ruined it all.

She felt a warm hand on her arm and turned. "Are you okay?" Nick asked.

She brushed away the tears. "Not yet. I'm sorry, Nick."

"I don't know what you're talking about, but you have nothing to be sorry for." He sat next to her and turned to look at her face. "While you're here, you should have that bruise x-rayed, make sure nothing's broken."

"I should have told the lieutenant about the group sooner. They might have found the suspect by now. I hope he hasn't gotten away."

Nick shook his head. "I doubt that." He wrapped his arm around her and pulled her close.

"Don't, Nick. I don't want the lieutenant to see."

He looked into her eyes, and she felt the love that had evaded her all these years. "I know I should care if he did, Sarah, but I don't anymore. There's more to life than a job."

"You've put so much into this department, Nick. I don't want to mess it up for you."

He let her go. "I think you'll be surprised at how much is going to change around Fossil Creek PD, Sarah. You're part of the team. It wasn't just you or me working this. It was the entire department. The city is pretty involved, too. If criminals reacted logically, we wouldn't have jobs. Speaking of which, we need to ask your sister some questions. I think she'd be more comfortable with you there."

He took her hand and led her from the pew, then

paused in the aisle. "This may have to last us awhile," he whispered as he bent his head toward her.

She raised her arms and wrapped them around his neck, gazing up at him. "I've waited fourteen years. I'll probably survive on this for a long time."

His kiss was slow and gentle, giving her hope that she wouldn't have to wait long for the next one. Their lips had barely parted when he kissed her again, playfully, teasing a smile from deep inside her heart.

Lieutenant Douglas and Detective Wang met with Sarah and Beth in an available office at the hospital. Nick stood in the doorway of the crowded room as they asked difficult questions. Sarah didn't like hearing her thoughts come out of another officer's mouth, but she knew they had to be asked.

"Why was your fiancé at your house, Miss Roberts?"

Sarah felt the pain hearing their suspicions caused her sister. "Remember that these questions are standard, Beth," she said softly, hoping to alleviate the sting.

"I decided you were right," Beth admitted. "That Sarah was right—I had to be honest. I needed to tell him about the attack. He said he was going to make the guy pay if he came back," she said, whimpering. "I guess he was watching the house or something."

Sarah glanced at Nick and shared a look of concern as the officers asked more intimate questions about their relationship. Finally, Beth got mad. "I hear what you're asking. No, there's no way Steve could be the rapist. He's as strong in his beliefs as I am. We each made this decision on our own, long ago. It's never been an issue for either of us. When we started getting serious, we made this commitment to each other."

Sarah was proud of how Beth handled the questions. "Besides, Steve has curly, dark brown hair. The man who attacked me had fair coloring and a buzz cut. Hasn't that been the same with all of us who were attacked?"

Detective Wang nodded. "We need to ask, Beth, to make sure that when prosecutors get you to the stand, they can't turn the question against you. If we don't ask, it leaves your testimony open for interpretation. We're very sorry this is so difficult."

"Did you tell Steve that your sister was going to look for your flash drive?" Douglas asked.

"I didn't know they were going over there," Beth replied. "We had all agreed—Sarah, my parents and me—not to be there after dark. We'd left about five o'clock to be sure."

They asked her more technical questions before having Nick walk her back to the waiting room to her parents and Steve's family. "Miss Roberts, it goes without saying that you shouldn't travel anywhere alone," Wang cautioned just before she left.

She nodded, giving Sarah a glassy-eyed glare. "Don't worry. I won't be going anywhere alone for a long time."

"Officer Roberts," the lieutenant said, "I need to talk to you, in private."

Detective Wang left.

Nick was gone.

She was alone with her supervisor, looking down the barrel of her future. A career that she'd worked hard to excel in.

"We've been very impressed with your investigation skills, Sarah. I can appreciate how difficult it has been to separate yourself from the case. I believe you'll agree that the best thing we can do to protect you and your sister is to place you on leave until the suspect is apprehended."

She could only stare at him. "What about a desk position?"

"This is nondisciplinary, Sarah. The chief and I have no intention of letting you go, but your safety as well as your family's has been greatly threatened, and we don't want any mental duress to impair a conviction. I know you wouldn't want it to end up being thrown out."

"Of course not." She froze in place.

"We'd like to suggest you and your sister consider—"

"I highly doubt you'll get her to leave Steve," Sarah interjected. "I'm not going to leave *her,* either." She handed him her badge and weapon. "Just in case, I want to remove any doubt that I'm acting as part of the department."

"What's this for?" He frowned. "I don't want these, Sarah."

"When the case is solved, I'll be honored to wear the badge again, Lieutenant. In the meantime, I have my family to care for."

Sarah was trembling. She hadn't meant to do that. But it was the only way she could keep from hurting Nick's or her own career.

TWENTY

Nick sat in the hospital lobby with Sarah's family, silently wondering how to keep the two sisters safe. The message on Beth's dresser mirror haunted him. "You're next."

So the culprit obviously knew where Beth lived. Was that because they were acquaintances, or because he'd stalked her? Did he also know Beth's sister? Where she lived? Would they be safe there? Mr. Roberts had been in the military, but what training had he had? How well prepared was he to defend his family? How much longer could he stay and protect them?

Leaning forward, Nick propped his elbows on his knees. What was taking Sarah so long? She wouldn't confess her feelings for him to the lieutenant, would she?

He was positive that no one on the force had a clue how he felt about Sarah. He hadn't said anything to anyone about them. He'd barely acknowledged his feelings to himself. They'd agreed that it was way too soon to make any move to get closer. There was too much at stake for both of them.

God, help me handle this the right way. Help me know who I can trust, Lord. Is Sarah among them? Or am I blinded by my feelings for her? He took a deep breath. *Open my eyes to Your plans for me.*

"What's taking her so long?" her father asked, interrupting Nick's conversation with God. "Is she in trouble?" he asked pointedly.

"They're probably just discussing the incident," he said hopefully. He thought he knew Lieutenant Douglas well enough to be certain she wasn't in trouble. But a year ago, he'd felt sure he knew the officers who'd betrayed him, too.

He had to get on with his life. He knew that. He knew his aunt was right; he needed to take a chance and trust again. He'd taken a huge step, sharing his feelings with Sarah. Kissing her. Being willing to keep a confidence that could come back to hurt both of them.

Some betrayals went deeper than others. Having his honor questioned had been a blow he'd been totally unprepared for. This, he realized, was one of the many shadows he would have to deal with for the rest of his life—that shadow of doubt. He had needed to throw out the net and find out if he'd fall through, or if God would truly answer his prayers. He had prayed for truth to prevail in the trial, and it seemed that God had answered his prayers. Charges against him had been dropped.

So why was he still waiting for the worst to happen? Why did he still question whether he would be strong enough to make the right decisions at the right times?

A yellow chicken costume flashed through his mind—Sarah, lying on the ground, the rape suspect kicking her….

Nick wasn't sure he'd pass this test. The incident at the festival—seeing her hurt—had rattled him.

Confirming that his partner was fighting the same feelings toward him as he was her had shaken him.

Kissing her, though—*that* had been what had knocked him off his feet. Now he wondered if it would be the final blow to his career.

Was he really in love? Or was that, too, another test?

It wasn't two minutes later when Sarah appeared at his side. "I'm sorry I took so long," she said. "I was arguing with the lieutenant," she whispered. "I turned in my badge and weapon…." She looked right at Nick.

His jaw fell. "You what?" That was the only question he could voice publicly, of the dozen others he wanted to ask the pint-size powerhouse. *What are you thinking?* was next on the list. *Have you lost your mind?* ranked high up there, too. "Why?"

"Sergeant Matthews," Lieutenant Douglas said as he walked into the waiting room, holding Sarah's weapon and badge. "We need to talk," he ordered. "Meet me downtown."

Shadows of doubt closed in around Nick. He looked at Sarah, who had tears brimming in her eyes as she glanced toward her sister. "Yes sir, I'll be right there," he said.

As soon as his supervisor left, he turned back to Sarah, leading her to a seat in a quiet corner. "Why?" was all he said.

"I can't risk my badge, Nick. Honor is far more important than a job. I have to get to the bottom of this. You know the rest," she said softly, glancing toward her parents, but ignoring their curious perusal. "Call me later. I doubt I'll get much sleep today."

He nodded. "You shouldn't go through with the move today, Sarah. Not until we catch this…creep," he said quietly. "I don't want to take the chance of him following you." He longed to hold her and protect her, to shut out all the betrayal that seemed to surround them.

She closed her eyes and nodded. "I don't think any of us will be in shape to move anything now. There's a lot to think about. I need to get more information from the Web, to stop this sicko before he hurts anyone else. I couldn't, in good conscience, pay full attention to that when I'm wearing the badge, Nick."

"No, you shouldn't be doing it at all," he whispered, mindful of the questioning glances her parents were sending them. "I need to go, Sarah." He patted her shoulder. "You call me anytime. Especially today. We need to discuss what happened with the lieutenant."

She nodded. "It was my idea, Nick. He argued with me not to turn in my badge. We didn't talk about what may happen after the rapist is caught…whether I can come back. I just know I had to do this. I understand now why God brought me back here…." She rubbed her eyes, which were once again leaking tears.

"I'll be sure to add an extra dose of thanks to my prayers today, then." He understood what she wasn't saying. They were frighteningly alike that way, and it had nothing to do with the few weeks they had been patrolling together.

"I'd call you in five minutes if I could, but since you'll be in with Lieutenant Douglas, why don't you phone me when you get home? I don't care what time it is."

An hour later Nick was still in the lieutenant's office, evaluating the events of the evening, assessing the call at the festival and the situation at Sarah's sister's house.

"Roberts turned in her badge. Any idea why?" Douglas asked at last.

"I was as surprised as you were. All along, she's been mindful of the lines she had to draw with her sister's assault case. Tonight must have been the final straw. I'm not sure."

The lieutenant studied him in silence. "Did she seem like she was losing control?"

Nick said another quick prayer for wisdom. "She's as human as the rest of us, sir. This has been a difficult situation, yet Officer Roberts has maintained a high level of professionalism throughout these cases. She's following all limitations and standards of the department. When she's revealed new information, she's passed—"

"That's more than I asked for, Matthews. A simple 'no' would have been fine."

His lip twitched even though he tried to stop it before the lieutenant noticed. "No, she's not lost control any more than any of the rest of us would have in her shoes."

"Good," Douglas said, then went on to discuss strategy for locating the rapist. "Much as I hate to involve her, especially as an unauthorized investigator, Officer Roberts has shared her intention to start looking on her own. And she's far closer than our detectives are to figuring this out."

"You're not going to allow her to—"

"Of course I'm not. She's not an officer anymore, Nick. She's a citizen protecting her family. You know how dangerous it could be to leave any of them out there alone. And I don't want you an easy target, either. I'm personally going to oversee this investigation."

Nick tried to keep his composure. "You're letting her get more deeply involved?"

"You have a better idea?" the lieutenant asked. He rattled off a list of damages not only to the victims, but to commerce and tourism in town. "No one wants to leave their houses this month. This conference promises to bring in much-needed revenue, and we need to prevent anything from happening. The safety of our citizens is our number one priority."

Nick didn't dare comment. Wang wasn't the best investigator for a computer case, but he should have been able to handle it better than this, what with the computer help that he'd been given. "What do you have as far as victims filing charges?"

"Nothing. They've all backed down."

Nick didn't like the sounds of that. "All of them? Didn't they at least I.D. the suspect?"

"Same description, nothing else. There's one DNA sample, from the first victim, but it won't be delivered until after the new year, most likely. She doesn't want the baby to have any clue how it was conceived. She's searching for an adoptive family, has moved out of state, and wants nothing to do with any court case."

Nick shook his head.

The lieutenant continued, "So we have our strongest evidence out of the picture. The victim who escaped any harm—any serious physical harm, anyway—is related to our best investigator at the current time. The neighbor is still refusing to get involved, since the suspect knows where she lives. Her landlord won't let her out of the lease for fear he'll lose half the block in tenants if she moves. She's still getting threats, and just wants to finish her degree. She's in her final semester, and hired a private bodyguard to protect her. Steve doesn't sound like he's going to be much help for a while." Douglas dropped his pen on his desk, as if giving up.

"What about the victim from the festival?"

"She wasn't assaulted, and isn't taking any chance of provoking the suspect. Like all the others, she felt safe at Coedspace. But no more. She's backed out of the conference already. I don't have to remind you that we know who he's after. And while Beth's fiancé is in critical condition, we're not going to get her out of harm's way."

Nick looked out the window at the bright orange sky as the sun rose. "We've been here twelve hours now. I wish I felt safe putting this to bed for the day, but I don't. That conference is only five days away.

"This guy has already changed his pattern to adjust to the conditions. Last night, he made a huge change, moving his attacks indoors. He left a definite message that he knows a lot about Beth, her life, her boyfriend.... He's attacked outside her workplace, outside her home. It was natural that the next place was going to be inside—and we weren't prepared. Nothing gets closer than inside her house. Inside her family."

Nick logged onto the Coedspace account Sarah had created for him, went into the archives and read Beth's blogs around the time of her attack.

"You're thinking he has to know about her sister?"

Nick nodded. "If he's watching, how can he miss it? Beth wrote a month ago about her excitement that her sister had moved here, her classes…her apologies to someone for having to come to class at night…." He paused, noting that last entry was a day before the attack. He scrolled back further. Who was the whiner?

Vgnwtchr726.

"So, is he a poor speller, or was he trying to convince them he was watching vegans?" the lieutenant said sarcastically. He pulled the case file from his desk and pointed to dates when the attacks had taken place. "The first was on April 26. A possible related attack has shown up on June 25, at almost midnight—maybe his watch was set fast? Beth's was August 26…. There was nothing on July 26?"

Nick knew it couldn't be that easy. "The neighbor was on September 3. But last night was only the 10th. If the '726' isn't his attack dates, what else could it be? That's close to Beth's house number, but not quite."

"Maybe it's our suspect's birthday. This is about him, in his eyes. He did say he likes the chase even more than the catch. He's playing…"

"A sick game. We do have access to the brain of someone with FBI experience. Don't you think it's time we talk openly with her about this?"

TWENTY-ONE

Sarah and her parents finally convinced Beth that she needed to come home and get some sleep after she'd been allowed to see her fiancé. They all felt a bit more secure, knowing a uniformed officer was stationed outside Steve's room.

Everyone else went upstairs to the bedrooms, except for Sarah. She went through the motions of making up the sofa as a bed and fluffing the pillow, but she knew she wouldn't be able to sleep. Not with the realization that, again, someone had suffered because she'd kept quiet. Still, just seeing the bed made up would make her mother feel better.

Sarah logged on to the computer, planning to dig for deleted files of Beth's instant messages. She needed to see what her sister had written to her online friends if she was going to be able to pose as Beth. While the computer started up, she made a list of things she had to do in preparation.

As soon as she logged on to the Web site as her sister, messages began popping up.

Hi, how're you doing? We missed you, from BlueDaisies.

Snobrdrocks asked where she'd been lately.

When will you have our assignments back? SusieSME inquired.

How did her sister have time for all of this, what with her own classes?

I hear you're moving, Wldncrzy wrote.

Sarah's instincts went into high gear. She had to come up with something to chat about to keep him on while she looked at his—or her—profile. Not by choice, she responded quickly, scanning for Wldncrzy's profile. She'd started typing more when he sent another message. She waited, erasing what she'd written.

Really? Why? Wldncrzy asked.

Having problems with some neighbors.

Yeah, that figures.

WonderDan sent her a message. Haven't seen you in a while. How about meeting for a cup of coffee?

Surely the rapist wouldn't use anything that could tie to his own name. His profile would be squeaky clean. Sorry, not today, she typed, clicking back to the other conversation.

Did you make it to the harvest festival? she asked, copying both on the message.

Before she got any reply, both said goodbye and logged off. That's fishy, she thought.

Sarah waited on the sofa, wondering if Nick had survived his meeting with the lieutenant. She hoped none of her actions would be taken against him. Just then, her phone rang.

"Hi," she said with a smile. "I'm glad you called."

"I'm outside. Is this a good time to talk?"

She jumped up and ran to open the door, closing her cell phone. "This is even better than hearing your voice on the phone," she told him.

He looked around to make sure they were alone. "May I come in?"

"Sure. Do you want some coffee?"

He smiled. "I didn't think you drank coffee."

"I don't, but I have it for my folks. Let me make a pot." She went into the kitchen and started digging through boxes.

"Don't worry about it, Sarah. I forgot you're still packed up."

"Since we're not moving today, it has to come out again, anyway." She continued with the quest, then returned her attention to him. "I'm sorry I threw a curve ball at you tonight, Nick. I was sitting there with the lieutenant and just realized I need to focus on my family. The abstinence conference is this weekend. We only have a few days to stop this guy."

"I agree with you. Wang would have nothing if

you hadn't handed the online ties to him. But more importantly, Sarah, I'm concerned that you stay safe. You can't go out there without backup."

She pulled the sheet and pillow from her sofa and motioned for him to sit down. Dropping them in a corner, she sat in the chair. "It's definitely a lot less comforting when I don't have the badge and the entire police force to back me, but I'll be careful."

He studied her, guessing that sitting across the room was a message that she wasn't ready to move on, despite the absence of protocol standing like iron bars between them. "Are you planning to return to duty?"

"Of course." Her eyes met his. "I mean, I hope to, if they're willing to hire me back after this case is closed."

"You didn't actually quit, did you?"

She looked at him, her eyebrows drawn into a V. "I haven't signed the paperwork, but I made it clear I didn't want—"

"Lieutenant Douglas doesn't make it sound like it's more than an administrative leave, to give you a breather to deal with a family issue. He's taking over the case. What else did you two discuss?"

"Are you working the case?"

"Not officially," Nick said, "but I have a very personal interest in your safety."

She stood up and paced the floor, with her hands

on her hips. "I turned in my badge to keep from hurting you, Nick. Letting you get involved is out of the question."

He said a silent prayer that God would help him trust Sarah—with his heart, his life and his career. Then he pulled her to him. "I'm already involved, Sarah. God willing, this isn't a temporary partnership. So what's going on?"

TWENTY-TWO

By the end of the week, Sarah had all but figured out exactly which screen name was responsible for the assaults. She just had to figure out his real name and find his real address. The Waiting for Marriage conference was going on as planned, with heightened security. Sarah had called her friend to fill in for the workshops her sister had planned to present.

Steve had been transferred to a hospital in Denver, and Beth went to stay with Joel so she could be closer to her fiancé. She hadn't taken two seconds backing out of the conference, and Sarah planned to show up looking like her sister, hoping their suspect would fall for the ruse.

Though they argued, Sarah convinced her parents to go visit Joel, too, and give her less to worry about while the police tried to close up the investigation.

She was getting used to thinking of herself and Nick in the present tense, even though they still hadn't come out in the open. When they weren't planning the investigation they were talking, making up for fourteen years.

Sarah closed on the condo, anxious to move in.

The lieutenant and Nick vetoed that idea, showing up together at her apartment one day. "Until he's in jail, I don't trust that our suspect's not out there watching your every move," Douglas said. "The chief has ordered us to put your apartment under surveillance, and you're not to go to your sister's without letting me know. We had the cable truck stop by to disconnect the service, but really, he put in a camera."

"I don't want to live with anyone watching me, whether it be FCPD or the assailant," she argued. "I can take care of myself, Lieutenant."

"Don't get difficult now, Roberts. It's not up for discussion," Douglas said emphatically.

Sarah lost the argument, again. Failure to get her own way didn't settle well. It seemed God was trying to beat submission into her head in every way.

Ten minutes later, the chief of police walked in with a box of wires and surveillance equipment. "After this case is settled, Officer Roberts, I'll be re-assigning you to help set up the department's online crimes task force."

Sarah looked at him, puzzled. "I didn't know FCPD had an online-crimes investigation unit."

"We will, as soon as you're there to set it up," the chief stated. "With your performance here, and your experience, it's a no-brainer."

The lieutenant broke in, drawing her attention back to the current crisis. "We've gotten another call from the suspect. He's threatening—promising is more like it, really—to find his next victim at the conference this weekend. We need to do something drastic, immediately."

"I'm not going to have just anyone watching me all week," Sarah said stubbornly. "I need people I've worked with. I want Nick to watch my back." She glanced at him, and the flicker of panic in his expression made her realize what she'd done. She had just asked to have him on her unit again.

"For this case, this week, that's fine," Douglas agreed. "But we need him back on the streets as soon as possible, so don't get used to the idea of taking him to the online unit with you."

Sarah felt a wave of relief, and could see from the look in Nick's eyes that he felt it, too.

The next twenty-four hours were spent going over the layout of her apartment, plus the grounds outside, and informing every player of all backup plans.

Sarah and the team went over everything meticulously, checking the mikes, cameras and earpieces. She sent an instant message to Nick on the Coedspace Web site to test their communications, then entered his phone number on speed dial on her cell and tested it.

"You're coming through okay, but you might review those notes I put in your mailbox last night," he said with a chuckle.

"You what?"

"See if you have the package I put in your mail slot last night. I thought it might keep you going through this week…." He added.

She thumbed through the pile of mail and found an extra set of handcuffs inside a candy tin. "Oh, you shouldn't have, Sergeant Matthews." Suddenly, she noticed this wasn't just another set of standard issue handcuffs. She gasped when she discovered a special key attached—and a delicate silver ring with a small heart design on it.

She could hear Nick laugh in her earpiece. "Read the note, too," he whispered.

"To a lifetime partnership, with God's blessings."

She fought back tears.

"Radio check," Nick said.

Sarah slipped the ring onto her left hand. "Affirmative," she managed to squeak.

"You ready to finish your disguise?" the chief asked. "We've set up a tail to follow you from the condo. If you need to go anywhere, let us know."

She put the fall wreath up on the door, pretending that life had never been better. Inside, though, she was tired of the act. She didn't like the feeling that strangers were watching her every move. She spent all her time on the computer, praying the assailant would soon take her bait and make his move. She was tired of trying to live someone else's life. It had only been two days and she was already getting cabin fever.

Finally, the suspect sent her an instant message, irate about her newest online article that true love didn't mind waiting until marriage.

"I'm going to run some errands. I'll be back in a couple of hours," she said into the wire that had become her constant companion.

"Need company?" Nick responded. She was beginning to read between the lines of what he said. She could hear his concern in each comment.

"No," she replied with a smile. "I'll be back well before dark. The bogeyman never strikes until nightfall." She could hardly wait to close this case so they could come clean with the chief.

Sarah went to the grocery store, then stopped in a nearby hair salon. If they were ever going to catch this guy, she had to look more like Beth. When the stylist called her to the back, she handed over a photo of her sister. "I want my hair to look like this."

An hour later, Sarah gazed in the mirror, stunned. She hadn't had short hair since she was a toddler.

She scanned the parking lot as she pulled up to

her apartment, not seeing any of the undercover officers. "Everything out here looks good. How're things in the house?"

"It's been quiet, except for the phone. Someone has been determined that you're going to answer," a man's voice said.

Sarah was puzzled by the change of guard. Why hadn't Nick told her he was leaving? Something wasn't right. "Where'd Nick go?"

"I'm not sure, but I think they had an emergency at the conference hotel. I was sent to watch your apartment." The man was speaking fast, and his voice wasn't familiar. She pulled out her cell phone to send a text message to Nick's number. The juniper bushes flanking her apartment looked like great hiding places, despite the outdoor cameras that should have alerted Nick to unexpected visitors.

"Any pizza left?"

"Sure," she said, realizing whoever she was talking to had to be in her apartment or else had seen the pizza delivery they'd had at noon. How had the suspect intercepted their frequency? "I'll send it up for a late-night snack," she said, playing along.

Sarah wasn't about to go inside until she knew who was waiting for her. "Oh, I forgot to pick up my mail. I'll be right in." She turned to get back into her car, but a blond-haired man matching the suspect's description cut her off.

TWENTY-THREE

She took off, but he caught up with her and shocked her with a Taser, knocking her to the ground. He dragged her to the porch of a neighboring building and immediately landed on top of her. She felt another electrical shock as he pressed the sharp point of a knife to her neck. "Hi, Sarah, or would you prefer I call you Beth?"

Sarah struggled to fight him off, but found she couldn't move. He'd obviously been trained to avoid all the failings they trained for in personal safety classes. She gasped for air. "We've—"

"Don't push your luck if you value your life. One word and you can join your sister's boyfriend in the morgue." He pressed the knife closer, reminding her that her life was in his hands. "I have a special room waiting for us, where no one will hear a thing."

Be my protector, Lord. She closed her eyes. *Deliver me from evil, God. Just give me one chance to bring him down. Give me strength to overpower him, to bring him to justice for what he's done to his other victims....*

Sarah wanted to scream, but she had to wait for him to remove the point of the knife from her jugular vein. She felt the ring on her finger and silently called out to Nick.

"Now, where'd they put your wire?" Her assailant shoved his hand up her blouse, furious to find no wires. He pushed away from her to continue the search.

Sarah kneed him in the groin as hard as she could. Too weak to continue to fight, she started praying again. *Dear God, save me from those who persecute me. Let justice be served.*

She heard shots fired, and his body fell onto her again.

"Sarah! Are you okay?" It was Nick's voice, raw and hoarse with fear.

She opened her eyes to see Nick standing over her, his soft gray eyes filled with desperation and fury. With his Glock still pointed at the suspect, he pushed him off of her with his boot then checked for a pulse. "He's dead." Other officers ran around the corner with weapons drawn.

Sarah closed her eyes and tried to roll away. Why couldn't she move? Was it the Taser? Or was it simply fear paralyzing her?

"Cover him, just in case," Nick ordered as he knelt next to her, pulling her blouse closed where the assailant had ripped the buttons loose. "Come here." He helped her sit up and drew her into his embrace, holding her tight. "Thank God you're okay."

She let her head rest on his shoulder. "I love you, Nick," she whispered.

Despite all the people around them, Nick murmured, "I love you too."

He was moving aside to let a medic examine her minutes later when he stopped to admire her short hair. "It looks good on you, but I barely recognized you—again."

She felt the chilly fall air blow down her neck. "At least it caught our suspect. Did you get any of what he said on tape—or did he cut your connection?"

"We lost it, but we have your testimony, and hopefully we can have Beth and Steve I.D. him," Nick said.

Sarah nodded. "I suspect we can get all of them to I.D. him now, even if it's no more than to reassure themselves that they're safe."

"Don't you scare me like that again." Nick wiped tears from her face.

"Don't worry, it's going to be a while before I'm ready for another decoy assignment." Sarah noticed her blouse and pulled her jacket closed, fumbling with the zipper. "Sitting behind a computer might actually be a nice change of pace," she said with a smile.

EPILOGUE

The last time Sarah had seen so many officers in uniform was at the funeral of a decorated hero after the attack on the Pentagon. Somehow, dress uniforms looked much better when they were worn with a smile.

The groom's smile as he gazed into the eyes of his bride gave Sarah hope that she'd one day be able to utilize Amber Scott's party planning services.

"Your sister is a beautiful bride," she whispered into Nick's ear.

"I can think of someone who'd look even prettier in a wedding gown." Nick's gaze didn't stray. "It's been six months, and I haven't heard anyone complain about us dating. What do you say we exchange that promise ring for the real thing?"

"You sure you can handle being married to a fellow officer?" she whispered. Her lips touched his and lingered there as the song ended.

When their lips parted, they realized the cheering wasn't for the bride and groom, but for them.

"Are you two trying to make an announcement?" his sister said with a smile. Kira and Dallas stood arm in arm, ready to throw the bouquet.

"Ten-four." Nick nudged Sarah. "Catch it."

"Yeah, right," she muttered, glancing at the two volleyball players up front. "I don't stand a chance with the twin towers over there."

"Don't worry, I've got you covered." Nick put his hands on her waist, and Sarah realized what he had planned as the screaming began. His hold tightened and he lifted her above the other bachelorettes as the flowers shot into the air. "Marry me, Sarah Roberts."

"Yes!" Sarah held her arms up, caught the bouquet, and cheered.

* * * * *

Ready for more Matthews brothers?
Look for Garrett's story,
SHIELD OF REFUGE,
coming in November 2008,
only from Love Inspired Suspense.

Dear Reader,

I can't tell you how blessed I am to write fiction, and how blessed that God has provided me with so many wonderful characters and their stories. You may be catching on that this series, In the Line of Fire, is very close to my heart. I've dedicated each story to one of my three children, in one way or another. While their names may be used to honor the blessings they've brought to my life, the stories are truly fiction. Praise the Lord that our real lives are nowhere near this exciting!

Sarah and Nick's story is about the deepest conflict that police officers can withstand, betrayal from those they trust. Yet that betrayal is not unique to men and women in uniform. It happens every day to people everywhere in their relationships, in their families and in their communities. Even Jesus was betrayed and struggled with the aftereffects. I loved that Nick realized that. I loved him for wanting to walk away, but not doing so. He knew that God was always there to listen and sympathize with his troubles and fears.

I hope you've enjoyed Sarah and Nick's adventure of finding their way through life's challenges, learning to take a chance again. If you'd like to contact me, you can e-mail me at:

csteward37@aol.com
or P.O. Box 200286, Evans, CO 80620.

God Bless,
Carol Steward

QUESTIONS FOR DISCUSSION

1. Broken trust is sometimes more damaging because it's as much an emotional pain as it is a physical pain. It's like comparing a skinned knee to a broken femur. So what are some of the bandages that we put on to keep from being hurt again?

2. What are some steps a person can take when trying to build trust in someone else? What are some of the things Sarah does to try to get Nick to trust her?

3. Nick felt betrayed by people he worked with and trusted. What are some ways he opens himself up to trusting others again?

4. Why is it so difficult for Nick to believe Sarah when she tells him she's not working for Internal Affairs? Do you think he acts irrationally? What would you do in Sarah's place if someone didn't believe your truths?

5. Sarah acts very self-confident in many ways, but there are a few times when she tries to disguise her true self. Do you think she was really as confident as she acted? Why or why not?

6. Many times we are afraid to voice our opinions or beliefs. Sarah is learning from past experiences when to speak up and when to be quiet. Have you ever had to make the choice to keep quiet about something rather than hurt someone? How do you think God feels about these kinds of "secrets"? How do you think Sarah's choice is a sign of her growing faith in God?

7. Much of Sarah's struggle is yet to come. She's a take-charge kind of woman who is afraid to let any weakness show. How do you think God could help her to balance the demands of her career and personal life?

8. Do you see a willingness by the end of the book for both Sarah and Nick to make the necessary changes in order to have a Christian marriage? Give a few examples of the alterations they'd need to make.

9. Nick is torn between his feelings for Sarah and his career. How often do you think people are forced to make difficult decisions that mean choosing between something uncertain and their income?

10. Is there a right and wrong way to make such a difficult decision? Do you believe Nick was right to handle it the way he did? Did you understand Sarah's reasoning for wanting to handle it the way she suggested?

11. Sarah turned to law enforcement after a crisis hurt someone in her own life. Do you believe that was a coincidence, or do you believe this career suited her? What other jobs do you think she would have excelled at?

12. Police work is dangerous and emotionally challenging work, and it is often difficult for couples to deal with the obligations of the job. How do you feel being a Christian would help, or hinder, a police officer's ability to carry through with his or her duties? How do you think it could help to have a spouse who is also in law enforcement rather than some other line of work?

REQUEST YOUR FREE BOOKS!

2 FREE RIVETING INSPIRATIONAL NOVELS
PLUS 2 FREE MYSTERY GIFTS

YES! Please send me 2 FREE Love Inspired® Suspense novels and my 2 FREE mystery gifts (gifts are worth about $10). After receiving them, if I don't wish to receive any more books, I can return the shipping statement marked "cancel". If I don't cancel, I will receive 4 brand-new novels every month and be billed just $4.24 per book in the U.S. or $4.74 per book in Canada, plus 25¢ shipping and handling per book and applicable taxes, if any*. That's a savings of over 20% off the cover price! I understand that accepting the 2 free books and gifts places me under no obligation to buy anything. I can always return a shipment and cancel at any time. Even if I never buy another book, the two free books and gifts are mine to keep forever.

123 IDN ERXX   323 IDN ERXM

Name	(PLEASE PRINT)	
Address		Apt. #
City	State/Prov.	Zip/Postal Code

Signature (if under 18, a parent or guardian must sign)

Order online at www.LoveInspiredSuspense.com
Or mail to Steeple Hill Reader Service:

IN U.S.A.: P.O. Box 1867, Buffalo, NY 14240-1867
IN CANADA: P.O. Box 609, Fort Erie, Ontario L2A 5X3

Not valid to current subscribers of Love Inspired Suspense books.

Want to try two free books from another series?
Call 1-800-873-8635 or visit www.morefreebooks.com

* Terms and prices subject to change without notice. N.Y. residents add applicable sales tax. Canadian residents will be charged applicable provincial taxes and GST. Offer not valid in Quebec. This offer is limited to one order per household. All orders subject to approval. Credit or debit balances in a customer's account(s) may be offset by any other outstanding balance owed by or to the customer. Please allow 4 to 6 weeks for delivery. Offer available while quantities last.

Your Privacy: Steeple Hill Books is committed to protecting your privacy. Our Privacy Policy is available online at www.SteepleHill.com or upon request from the Reader Service. From time to time we make our lists of customers available to reputable third parties who may have a product or service of interest to you. If you would prefer we not share your name and address, please check here. ☐

LISUS08R

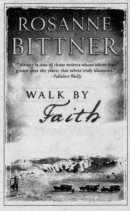

Love Inspired®
SUSPENSE

TITLES AVAILABLE NEXT MONTH
Don't miss these four stories in October

FORSAKEN CANYON by Margaret Daley

Kit Sinclair is determined to hike through Desolation
Canyon. Tribal chief of police Hawke Lonechief can't stop
her, so he agrees to lead her—on *his* terms. Hawke knows
the dangers the canyon holds...yet is he prepared for the
stalker dogging their steps?

COUNTDOWN TO DEATH by Debby Giusti
Magnolia Medical

Five people have contracted a rare, deadly disease. It's up
to medical researcher Allison Stewart to track down the
source. Research is one thing—defending her life is another!
Handsome recluse Luke Garrison comes to her aid. Still,
with the blame for an unsolved murder hanging over
Luke's head, Allison might be setting herself up to become
victim number six.

A TASTE OF MURDER by Virginia Smith

A beauty pageant judge is murdered—and Jasmine Delaney
could be next. She arrived in town for a wedding during
the Bar-B-Q festival. But when she fills in as a pageant
judge, the bride's brother, Derrick Rogers, fears she's the
next target. The killer has had a taste of murder. And is
hungry for more.

NOWHERE TO RUN by Valerie Hansen

Her former boyfriend told her to run...so she did. And
now the thugs who killed him are after Marie Parnell and
her daughter. Stuck with car trouble in Serenity,
Arkansas, Marie dares to confide in handsome mechanic
Seth Whitfield—who has some secrets of his own.

LISCNM0908